He Loves Me Not

Caroline B. Cooney

SCHOLASTIC INC
New York Toronto London Auckland Sydney

Cover Photo by Owen Brown

ISBN 0-590-40346-X

12 11 10 9 8 7 6 5 4 3 2   9/8 0 1/9

He Loves Me Not

A Wildfire Book

WILDFIRE TITLES
FROM SCHOLASTIC

Love Comes to Anne by Lucille S. Warner
I'm Christy by Maud Johnson
That's My Girl by Jill Ross Klevin
Beautiful Girl by Elisabeth Ogilvie
Superflirt by Helen Cavanagh
A Funny Girl Like Me by Jan O'Donnell
Just Sixteen by Terry Morris
Suzy Who? by Winifred Madison
Dreams Can Come True by Jane Claypool Miner
I've Got a Crush on You by Carol Stanley
An April Love Story by Caroline B. Cooney
Dance with Me by Winifred Madison
One Day You'll Go by Sheila Schwartz
Your Truly, Love, Janie by Ann Reit
The Summer of the Sky-Blue Bikini
     by Jill Ross Klevin
I Want to Be Me by Dorothy Bastien
The Best of Friends by Jill Ross Klevin
The Voices of Julie by Joan Oppenheimer
Second Best by Helen Cavanagh
A Kiss for Tomorrow by Maud Johnson
A Place for Me by Helen Cavanagh
Sixteen Can Be Sweet by Maud Johnson
Take Care of My Girl by Carol Stanley
Lisa by Arlene Hale
Secret Love by Barbara Steiner
Nancy & Nick by Caroline B. Cooney
Wildfire Double Romance by Diane McClure Jones
Senior Class by Jane Claypool Miner
Cindy by Deborah Kent
Too Young to Know by Elisabeth Ogilvie
Junior Prom by Patricia Aks
Saturday Night Date by Maud Johnson
Good-bye, Pretty One by Lucille S. Warner
He Loves Me Not by Caroline B. Cooney

1.

The phone call that changed my life came when I was just two days past fifteen, and it came from a twenty-seven-year-old saxophone player. I remembered him only because one month ago he had frowned at me the whole time I played the piano.

It was a dance at the community center: very casual, completely ordinary — no dates, just drop-ins. We danced mostly to records people had brought with them, but then somebody wanted "Autumn Leaves," and of course nobody had brought a record of that, so I played it on the piano. Then somebody else wanted Scott Joplin's "The Entertainer" and then "Moon River," and what with one request after another I played steadily for at least half an hour.

All that time this fierce, tough-looking character slouched in the doorway and frowned at me. Pretty soon I had the idea that people were gathering around the piano more for protection from this thug than to hear my music. The dance chaperons went over to him, presumably to inquire about his intentions, and he burst out laughing and left.

It turned out he was our friend David's big brother, who had driven David down to the dance since none of us had drivers' licenses yet.

"He frowned at you because you're a good musician," said David. "Ralph always frowns when he's impressed. It's when he grins you know you've made an idiot of yourself." David's face grew sad. "My brother grins at me more than he frowns," David confided.

Which made me feel very good about a solid half-hour of frowns.

I intended to become a professional musician, specializing in the harpsichord and keyboard music of the French Renaissance. I was saving my baby-sitting income to buy a harpsichord kit and build myself one, so I wouldn't have to practice at my teacher's. It is very inhibiting to do all your practicing with your teacher in the next room yelling that you got your trill backwards. I had seven hundred and twelve dollars to go before I could order the kit. Which would then take six months to arrive. And six months to build. But that was before the phone call.

"Alison?" said Ralph. "This is David's brother. Remember me? I heard you play at that kid dance at the community center."

The way he said "kid dance," he managed to imply that I, like Ralph, was no kid. I grinned into the phone. "Sure, I remember you. David told me you're a sax player."

"Right. Now listen. You knew what you were doing and I'm going to take a chance on you. My keyboard man has just come down with a bad case of flu. I drove to his apartment to haul him off to a wedding reception we're doing and he's so sick he can't even remember what instrument he plays. Can you be ready in twenty minutes to substitute for him?"

I flung on my Sunday dress: pale blue dotted Swiss with little tracks of white bows down the front. I grabbed a pile of piano music that looked as if it might have something wedding-y in it and was ready to run out to the curb when Ralph's van arrived. My father took one look at Ralph, panicked, and decided to come along. Ralph grinned at me. He had the fishiest grin I ever saw. No wonder David preferred his frown. I looked down at myself to see what was the matter. "Change your clothes," said Ralph. "Something dramatic. You want to look at least old enough to get paid."

Ralph was making me more nervous than the prospect of playing in public for one hundred wedding dancers. "I don't have anything dramatic," I said, thinking of my closet full of oxford shirts and Shetland sweaters.

"Then something invisible. Black pants and a black turtleneck, maybe?"

He had to settle for white pants and a white turtleneck. I did not feel invisible. I felt fluorescent.

On the way over, Ralph said, "I don't usually fool around with infants. Just remember to be a musician first and a fifteen-year-old second."

"Yes, sir," I said.

"It's bad for my image to be called sir," Ralph told me.

"What's your image?" said my father. He was

3

clutching the door, the seat, and the seatbelt to avoid being hurtled out of the van. Obviously Ralph did not intend to be late to this wedding reception.

"Music can be macho," said Ralph.

I was feeling about as far from macho as I ever had in my life. My fingers were so stiff with nervousness that I felt more like a reptile. I was growing a leather skin. We puffed into the country club dance hall with exactly two minutes to spare. The other members of Ralph's music group shook hands with my father and welcomed him to their combo. They nearly passed out when Daddy said, "I'm just along for the ride. Alison's your musician."

They actually scanned the room for a musician named Alison.

"That little girl?" said the trumpeter, Alec, as if praying to be told another Alison — an older, tougher, more experienced Alison — was going to pop out of the piano bench.

"She's okay," said Ralph. "Sit down, Alison. Start playing."

"Playing what?" I said, sitting down.

"Ralph," said the string base player, a very laidback woman named Lizzie, "she looks like a malnourished hitchhiker."

"We don't have time for an analysis of Alison's height and breadth," said Ralph coldly. "You know 'Some Enchanted Evening,' infant?" he said to me.

"Yes."

"Fine. In F. Give us a four measure intro."

And it all began: the wedding reception, the

4

music, the tension, the terrible nerves — and my career.

The only group I'd ever played with before had included a cello, two violins, and a viola, and we'd practiced for two months with our conductor before we even started to think about a public performance. This wedding reception was quite a contrast. It was both the most frightening and the most companionable experience of my life. Whatever their feelings about my age and competence, the other members of the combo set about making the music work. Ralph on sax, Lizzie on string bass, Rob on drums, and Alec on trumpet were like a quartet of lifesavers keeping the piano player from drowning.

After what seemed like a decade or so, Ralph said, "Nice. Take a break, Alison."

"I'm already broken," I said.

They laughed, and incredibly, wonderfully, I was a member of the group.

Ralph, of all things, was a pharmacist who was a partner in his father's drugstore. Evenings and weekends he ran a pool of musicians who supplied most of the music in our city. He handled any job from supper club dances to strawberry festivals, from bar mitzvahs to Junior League gatherings. He produced music that ranged from hard rock to Lawrence Welk, from ballads to Beatles to polkas.

The keyboard man with the flu turned out to have mono. He was in the hospital for weeks and then at home for weeks, and after that he was just not very interested in trying to keep two careers going. Pretty soon I was the one trying to keep two careers going: school, in which I had to do well because I had to be able to qualify for college scholarships, and Ralph's assignments, in which I had to do well for my own musical pride — and to keep Ralph from throwing me out in favor of someone older and more experienced.

Basically, my skill — at least the one Ralph cares about — is that I can memorize. Let me hear a piece twice on a record and I have it in my fingers. Let me read it once off a sheet or a chart and I've got it down.

I love working with the group. There's a tightness and a looseness to it; we work so closely together, and so easily. It's kind of exhilarating, as if every gig is a competition and we're always the winners.

Don't you think "gig" is the funniest word? It means a music job. My father says he thinks it comes from "giggle" because it seems so funny to Daddy that anybody would pay us to have so much fun! For quite a while my father went along with us, which bothered me much more than it bothered Ralph (Ralph is not easily bothered, except by musical incompetence), but then Daddy decided Ralph could be trusted with his little girl.

It was the night of the Lindsays' party — a whole year and a half after my first gig with Ralph — that I first really thought about what I was giving up in exchange for what I was getting.

Mr. and Mrs. Lindsay had spared no expense in celebrating their daughter's engagement. Since it fell on Valentine's Day, they had decorated their enormous house in a symphony of pink satin and white lace, silver ribbons and red roses. I could hardly play the piano, because I was staring at the guests, who were beautifully and formally dressed. Even the food had been cut in valentine shapes, from the tiny sandwiches to the enormous, magnificent cake.

"Alison," said Ralph in his sweetest voice, which is also his most dangerous, "you're being paid, love. Try to find the beat, please. They're going to break their ankles dancing to the selection you're playing."

I pulled my eyes from the group of young men coming in the door and put my attention on the keyboard. Ralph was right. I was rushing with my right hand and dragging with my left. The dancers were getting that uneasy look of people who are thinking about sitting down.

We wrapped up "Smoke Gets in Your Eyes" and drifted into "Misty" and "Stormy" and "Raindrops" and "I Love a Rainy Night." Finally Alec said, "Hey, Ralph, we're all going to mildew in this lousy weather of yours, man," and Lizzie said, "Try to remember they got engaged, Ralph, they're *happy*," and Ralph said, "Oh, yeah, okay, how about 'I'm in the Mood for Love'?"

Even the piano was festooned with pink and silver. It was a beautiful old Baldwin grand — glistening, dark, satiny wood — and on top was a huge, lovely bouquet of carnations and baby's breath. We'd had to shift it precariously so we could see each other, and every few numbers Ralph sidled around the piano to shove the vase back from the edge.

Out on the floor, dancing couples swayed and laughed and held hands and toasted each other.

Much as I love being a musician, it would be very, very nice — just once — to be a guest. To

7

have a date. To have a dance partner. To laugh with carefree delight instead of knotting up because I just mangled the repeat.

"Okay, infant," said Ralph, who for some reason always addresses me instead of the group. "Break time, kid. Good job. They love you."

I sagged on the bench. The dancers came reluctantly to a stop. I saw the bride-to-be and her fiancé drift slowly off the floor, but one future bridesmaid didn't feel like stopping; she and her boyfriend kept right on dancing until someone tapped them on the shoulder. They looked around, startled, and everybody laughed.

When am I ever even going to meet a boy? I thought, let alone dance with one? I'll spend my whole life on the bench while all the good ones dance on by.

I stood up, hungry and thirsty. Maybe one of the really good-looking young men who'd come in unattached would notice me at the buffet and romance would strike.

I have three outfits I wear to gigs, depending on what Ralph thinks is appropriate. This one was white velveteen trousers and a white satin blouse with lovely lace ruffles on the sleeves and down the front. I'm so slim I can always use a little fluff there, and the blouse is really becoming. I have rather long, dark hair, and for this party I'd done it ornately, with sequins and ribbons. I had on a pink sash, and Mrs. Lindsay had pinned a corsage of pale pink roses on me.

I felt smashing.

I've felt that way before, though, and no handsome young man has given the slightest sign of being smashed by me. Sometimes I feel as if the piano is attached to me, so that even when I'm not on the bench I look unavailable. The way some people look boring and others look sophisticated, I think I look *employed*.

The buffet turned out not to be a fraction as promising as Mrs. Lindsay had told us it would be. One thing I have found out for sure in the last year and a half: I have very low class, indeed peasant, tastes in food. I'll take a hot dog and cole slaw any time. The Lindsays, however, were fond of artichoke hearts, anchovy spread on pumpernickel squares, and asparagus on health crackers. I circled the buffet twice, but it didn't improve from any angle.

Three people — none of whom could possibly be classified as romantic young men — paused in loading their cupid-decorated plates with sardines and olives to tell me how much they were enjoying the music and I was awfully young, wasn't I?

I nodded mutely.

I am far more articulate with notes than with words. Ralph says if I could improvise with my tongue the way I do at the keyboard, I'd have the world by the tail. Lizzie says it only takes practice and if I would just open my mouth and try, eventually I'd learn the art of conversation.

I dipped the ruffled potato chip into a bowl and discovered the dip was something horrid and fishy. I buried the chip surreptitiously under a puffy crepe-paper valentine. By that time the adults had moved on, and my chance to improve my speaking abilities was gone.

I looked around forlornly for a slice of pizza or a peanut-butter-and-jelly sandwich, but there was nothing edible on the whole buffet. The average age of the partygoers was roughly twenty-two (the bride's friends) and fifty (her parents'). I hung around the buffet hoping some male twenty-two-year-old would pass by, and some did, but their eyes were on the caviar, not me. I have no use for people who eat fish eggs, anyway.

Ralph came between me and the punch and handed me a can of 7-Up. His second promise to my father is that soda is the strongest liquid I can drink. The first promise is that if Ralph thinks there will be grass or coke at a party, he's to take one of his other keyboard players and not me. Once Ralph misjudged, and when the party turned out to be wall-to-wall marijuana, he actually phoned my father to come and get me. I didn't know whether to be glad or furious. The result of that phone call, of course, is that Daddy thinks Ralph is the most admirable man in the city. (Ralph agrees with this analysis and quotes my father at every opportunity.)

"About tomorrow's gig," said Ralph, taking my share of punch as well as his own. "I know you need money, infant, but I talked to the host, and it's going to be a lot more wild than I figured when I signed you up for it. So forget it. I'll get somebody else."

Actually, I was delighted. I had a term paper to do for biology and desperately needed an entire day in the library. "Term papers," said Ralph, making horrible faces. "Just when I'd almost forgotten what an infant you are. Still in school worrying about grades."

"How old are you, dear?" said an elderly lady dressed in a shimmering golden sheath. I'd like to look that good *now,* let alone when I'm eighty.

"Sixteen," I said.

"My goodness! And you play so well, dear."

I never know how to handle compliments. I blush and shift my feet like a horse pawing the ground. "Thank you," I said. Lizzie says when in doubt just say thank you. She's right, it never fails.

"May I make a request?" the lady said, smiling shyly.

"Certainly," Ralph told her, half-bowing.

For what they're paying, I thought, he should kneel!

My stomach knotted up, waiting to hear the lady's request. With older people I hardly ever know the song, although, of course, after a year and a half of this I'm a lot better than I was. But playing a good smooth rendition of a song you don't know is quite a trick. Ralph gives me the key, the beat, and the tempo. Then I lay out an intro, and from there on I have to follow the others at the very same moment I'm actually playing: feeling the chords coming *before* we get there. It's very, very hard.

And yet, I always hope for tough requests. It's like fighting a lot of tiny wars; every evening is much more exciting if there's a skirmish to win. I wish I felt that way about school.

" 'My Blue Heaven,' " she said. "It's my favorite."

Sure enough, I'd never heard of it.

"I love it, too," said Ralph, who always says that even when he hates it and said last week if he ever had to play it again, he'd lose his sanity. I went back to the piano while Ralph talked to the lady, and meanwhile Alec (the trumpeter) hummed the tune for me, and Rob (the drummer) tapped out the rhythmic motif.

We went through it once with Alec taking the melody. Then, figuring I was secure with the chords, Ralph picked the tune up on his sax and really played around with it; it took all my concentration and energy to do my part. When we paused, what I wanted most was a nap, but the other guests had realized this was a request number and they began making requests, too. It was like being hit by a machine gun.

I didn't make any errors the audience knew about, although Alec gave me a dirty look once over the top of his trumpet and Ralph smiled in such a way that I knew if I didn't shape up I'd be replaced.

I shaped up. Ralph rewarded me with a fierce frown.

People don't think of music as being physically hard to do, but to me it is. When the Lindsay party was over I had to totter out to Ralph's van.

Sometimes I think the hardest part of performing comes when the gig is over. You're wound up so tight, you're so pleased with yourself, you're so exhausted — but you can't just shrug it off and go home and sleep. What you really need is an hour to celebrate the performance and exchange stories (". . . and when they asked for 'Mighty Like a Rose,' I nearly died . . ."). But all of us in Ralph's combo have to get up in the morning. We quit, we pack up, we mutter good-byes, and we leave.

Ralph drives me home, waits in his van with his headlights shining on my porch until I'm safely inside, and then he goes off. My father, who has been dozing, yells, "Is that you, Alison?" and I yell, "Yes, Daddy." Then he falls asleep and I stand there.

For the hundredth time that year, I'd come home from a party . . . alone.

It was the irony of my life.

I had the busiest social schedule of any girl at senior high — and I had never had a date.

I spent weekend after weekend at parties, dinners, socials, dances, and receptions — and I had never received an invitation. Never danced, never sat down at a meal, never had an escort (unless you count Ralph; my father certainly counts Ralph), and never had my hand held (except by the combo; they certainly felt I got my hand held a lot).

I took a long shower, letting the hot water drain the tension of the evening out of me. My mind ran over the things I'd done well as well as the mistakes I'd have to correct and the practice I'd need to do.

And mixed in with all the pride and the pleasure at being a good musician doing a good professional job was loneliness. I didn't have a single person to share it all with.

I went to sleep wondering what it would be like to go to a party as somebody's girlfriend, instead of somebody's keyboard player.

2.

"Tell me about it," I begged Frannie. "Come on. Please?"

Frannie just shook her head and laughed, as if I were making a really ridiculous request. She fiddled with the pages of her American History assignment. We were studying election regulations and trends. "It was a silly date, Alison," she said. "It was nothing. We just kind of walked around. You know you aren't interested in that. Now tell us about the Lindsays' party. I was thinking about you Saturday night. They have such a super house. That marvelous curving brick drive and that beautiful portico with all the white pillars. Like Cinderella or something. That must have been some dance!"

"I hear they actually have a ballroom right in the house," said Lisa. "Is that true, Alison? I mean, it is a big house, but it doesn't look large enough to have a real ballroom."

"Oh, tell us about it!" cried Jan. "Suzanne

14

Lindsay's picture was in the newspaper and she looked absolutely beautiful. I bet you had a super time, didn't you, Alison?"

"It was okay. Just a dance. The decorations were nice, though." I wanted to hear about Frannie's date. Her little brother Joey had sold the most candy bars of anybody in his elementary school, raising money for playground equipment. But the day they had to be delivered, Joey was throwing up, so Frannie waded through ice and slush and old blackened snow to make the deliveries for him. And who should volunteer to walk with her but Dick Fraccola! I'd love to go anywhere with Dick, especially laughing our way through the snow with a box of candy bars.

"It was okay," Jan mimicked me. "Just a dance." She and Frannie and Lisa rolled their eyes at each other. "Miss Jet Set here can't even be bothered to describe the party of the season."

"Aftah all, dahling," said Frannie, affecting an accent, "they're such a *bore* when you're out night after night."

I often wondered what they thought I did at these parties. Did they really see me as Cinderella, taking the social scene by storm? I'd told them often enough that for me these parties were work, but they never seemed to hear me. They always thought I was just being a pain.

"Did you wear your scarlet satin number?" said Lisa.

"No, that's too gaudy for an engagement party," I said. "At an engagement party the bride is the star and the musicians have to be pretty low-key. I wore my white velveteen costume."

"Gosh, I envy you," said Lisa, and from her voice I thought she really did. "The most exciting party I've ever been to was Halloween, bobbing for apples at Kevin's house."

I'd never been to Kevin's. He gave a lot of casual parties. They had a big basement with an old jukebox, a pinball machine, a few electronic games, and of course a good stereo set; the kids went there a lot. You knew you were *in* if you dropped in at Kevin's a lot. Kevin had asked me. Once. I'd had to decline. I remember the occasion vividly, because I had felt so completely stupid. "Oh, Kevin," I said, "I'd love to!" I proceeded to drop all my books trying to pull out my engagement calendar, and my Math book smashed Kevin's foot. "I'm sorry," I said desperately. "It's okay," said Kevin, "I only walk on the bottoms. Can you come?" I bent over to gather up my books, when a girl tripped over me and I went sprawling. After Kevin had gathered me *and* my books and relocated us in a corner, he said a third time, very patiently, "Can you come?"

I opened my calendar, and Kevin actually gasped at the list of activities I had there. What with term papers, exams, combo practice, music deadlines, and all the gigs Ralph had lined up, the calendar was pretty impressive. Just *looking* at my schedule exhausts me. I never see how I'm going to live through the month, juggling everything; and every time I turn over a new page I'm sort of amazed, and I think, I really did live through the month.

"I'm sorry," I said, and I was really, painfully, terribly sorry. "I have a dinner."

"Oh," said Kevin. "Well, have fun." He stacked my books carefully in my arms and pointed me toward my next class and he never asked me again.

The dinner was the induction of officers for the Junior League's new year. It was the most boring thing I ever endured — some of the gigs Ralph lines up can be pretty dull.

Sometimes, in the cafeteria line or at the school bus stop, Kevin mentions my schedule to someone. "Forget Alison," he says, although he's nice about it and smiles — as if he's proud of me. "She's probably tickling the ivories for the governor, or something."

And once Pete Fox asked me to go to the library and study with him. We had a huge, frightening test coming up in Biology: the skeletal, muscular, digestive, and reproductive systems of every little beast we'd studied. "I wish I could, Pete," I said, checking my calendar, "but I have a rehearsal."

"You can skip a rehearsal," said Pete. "You must know all that stuff cold by now."

"No," I said helplessly. "There's always a new hit to learn, or a different kind of music for an unusual gig. Smoothing out the rough spots from the last performance. Working out transitions. Spacing . . ."

But Pete was bored by that. And hurt, I think. He really thought there was no reason for me not to skip the rehearsal except that I didn't want to study with him.

The only person who agreed that I couldn't possibly skip a rehearsal was our football captain,

Michael MacBride, who said he personally liked to kill people who missed football practice. I said, "Gee, sort of cuts down on the lineup, doesn't it?" Mike laughed and touched my shoulder as he passed on, and that was the closest I have ever come to a boy-girl chat.

Furthermore, Pete Fox never quite forgave me for getting an A-minus on that Biology test when he got a C-plus. He was positive I'd skipped the rehearsal anyhow and studied by myself. I tried to describe how Lizzie and Alec quizzed me all through the practice. Ralph would say, "Okay, let's listen to that record again. Now get that modulation right this time, you jerks," and Lizzie would say, "Okay, Alison, what two kinds of ribs does a frog have?" After I'd listened very hard to the modulation I'd say, "Fused and carpel," and Alec would say, "Discuss the digestive system of the earthworm." Then Ralph would scream, "There's got to be a keyboard player somewhere who's out of high school!"

It was fun studying with the combo, but I'd far rather have studied with Pete Fox. After all, Lizzie, Rob, and Ralph are all in their twenties. (Alec is nineteen and rather spaced-out. He took a year off between high school and college to "find himself" and, as Lizzie says, he's finding less and less each week.)

But when I tried to tell Pete about the combo, he only got the idea that the combo was more fun for me than he was, and he went off bristling and annoyed and hurt.

I dragged myself out of my daydreams and listened to Jan and Lisa and Frannie going on and on about the Lindsay party. "Really," I said to them helplessly, "It wasn't that exciting. More than half the guests were Mr. and Mrs. Lindsay's age, or even older, and we did a lot of slow dances, waltzes, and foxtrots, and we didn't do much rock at all. We had requests going back to Jerome Kern and — "

"Forget the music," said Jan impatiently. "Tell us about the party!"

But for me the music had been the party.

"What did everybody wear?" demanded Jan. "What did the bride wear?"

I tried to remember what the bride had worn. I tried to remember something besides the awful buffet and that moment when Ralph smiled evilly at me. "There was this old lady in a golden sheath," I said finally.

"Sheesh!" said Jan, furious with me. "Don't be such a snob. Talk with us for a change."

The bell rang for classes and I had to go in the opposite direction from them.

Sometimes I felt that music, far from being the international language that binds everybody together, had become a wedge between me and my friends. Even the people I knew who were musical — played in the marching band or took piano lessons — didn't understand.

But then, I didn't know how to explain myself, anyway.

People asked me about it often enough. You'd think I would have found an easy, logical answer to describe me and music.

I watched Jan and Lisa and Frannie go off together and wondered what they were saying about me. I won't care about it, I told myself. I've bungled a lot of friendships and that's that. In two years, I'll be at college, I'll be a music major, I'll be with people who understand. Until then I'll just have to endure high school.

That sounded fine. It carried me about five steps down the hall toward Latin, when I saw, way ahead of me, a boy and a girl sneaking a quick kiss before breaking apart to go their separate ways for the next class.

Two years? I thought miserably. Hang in here alone for two whole years?

I had this overwhelming desire to have somebody love me for myself, not my fingers on the keyboard. To have somebody want to kiss me, not hear me play an old hit tune. I thought how much more warm and wonderful it would be to stroke a boy's hand instead of ivory, and then I felt absolutely stupid for thinking like that.

My footsteps were getting slower and slower.

The hallways cleared and in another moment I would be late.

Boys, I thought. I don't even have time to daydream like a normal person, let alone make friends and start dating.

It isn't worth it, I thought. I'll tell Ralph I'm quitting. I'm so lonely it hurts and music just isn't that important.

I scurried alone down the stairs to Latin.

3.

Latin used to be a forgotten subject. Nobody took it. But when I was in ninth grade, there were seventeen of us in first-year Latin and we all loved it. Not one of us dropped out. The class has the same sort of comradeship that the combo does: a tight, yet easy friendship that comes from sharing something difficult and special.

Unfortunately, I hadn't had time to do my translation, and with only seventeen people in the class you almost always get called upon daily.

"I see panic in your eyes," murmured Mike MacBride.

"I didn't have time to do the translation."

"Superwoman has fallen short. I don't believe it."

I flushed, but Mike was smiling at me. "I'm no superwoman," I said, embarrassed. And proved it. Miss Gardener called on me first and I couldn't even fake my way through the first noun.

"Zero," said Miss Gardener gladly. "Too many

activities, Alison. Too little attention to what counts, I'm afraid."

When other people had trouble, Miss Gardener helped them, rather gently. She'd ask for excuses and she'd accept them, no matter how thin they were. We were her favorite class. But when I failed she was glad. I spent the rest of Latin fighting tears.

After class, Mike tugged my hair. It was a funny thing to do. It sounds mean, but it wasn't. It was sort of affectionate. I looked up at him and thought that any time he wanted to show *more* affection, I'd be happy to cooperate! I tried to think of something clever to say but nothing came to me. I looked back down at my desk while I gathered up my books, wondering if he had seen my tears.

"It's just a dumb Cicero translation," said Mike, "not the end of the world."

He smiled at me and the world tumbled back into perspective. What a super thing a nice smile is! I felt warmed up like sunshine, and I hugged my books to my chest and smiled back. Mike tugged my hair again and walked on.

He was gone before I realized I had not said one word to him. A boy I really liked, who was nice to me, and I hadn't even tried to let him know I was glad he'd taken the time to speak to me.

I thought, I know about as much about boys right now as I did about gigs two years ago. Zero.

I began a long involved fantasy about how I would be deluged with offers of dates, so Ralph would have to get substitutes for me five nights a week, and my phone would be ringing off the hook with the deep, romantic voices of strange boys. My father would be meeting a new one at the door every night and I'd leave my spangled sheath at the dry cleaner's and stock up on all these frilly romantic little numbers. I'd dance instead of provide dance music and all the boys standing on the sidelines would turn and stare at me, the way they do in TV ads for women who have on a new brand of pantyhose.

I figure if you're going to have a fantasy, you should really lean into it and get it top-drawer.

I thought of the girl being kissed in front of her classroom and told myself that before long I'd have boys arguing over who got the thrill of kissing *me* in front of —

"Alison!"

Fantasies down the tube. It was a girl calling me.

"Alison!"

I turned to see who it was. Lucy, who moved to town about a week before I began playing for Ralph. Needless to say, I don't know her very well. We sit next to each other in Chem, though, and once in a while we meet in the cafeteria. She's one of these people you know you'd like tremendously if there were just time to be around her . . . but there's never time. Whenever Lucy talks to me or waves at me I feel a twinge. I want to ask her to spend the night or come over after school or something, but I never do because I never can. "Hi, Lucy," I said, beaming at her.

"Listen, I know how busy you are, and I'm almost afraid to ask, but I'm having a party for

Kathleen Devaney Saturday night and I'd love to have you come."

"Oh, I'd love to." I said. It was my refrain. I knew perfectly well I couldn't come Saturday night. Ralph had booked me to play for a dinner party. People who were paying a lot of money made arrangements weeks, if not months, in advance. And although I might quit playing for Ralph, I certainly couldn't quit when he had no replacement for me, not with three nights' notice.

Lucy had a calendar out — the tiny, pretty kind that Hallmark gives out free, where you have a quarter-inch of space per day to write in appointments. Fine, if you have to go to the dentist once and a party once. I felt pushy and ridiculous getting out my fat leather book and turning to Saturday to prove to Lucy I was really busy. Very busy.

"I'm really going to miss Kathleen, aren't you?" said Lucy mournfully. "When I moved here, Kathleen was all that stood between me and total loneliness. I want to give her a really special going-away party."

"Kathleen?" I said, stunned. "Kathleen's moving?" In first, second, and third grades Kathleen Devaney had been my very best friend. We used to alternate meals at each other's houses, and I couldn't begin to guess how many times she spent the night. The Devaneys moved across town in our fourth-grade year, so we'd been in different elementary and junior high schools, but we'd kept our friendship up. In senior high we were so glad to be together again that we used to hug each other in the halls.

Lucy burst out laughing. "Alison, you're so out of touch," she said. "Kathleen announced at least three months ago they were moving."

"Three months?" I said. And she hadn't called me. Hadn't said a word to me.

But then, when was the last time I'd called Kathleen? My heart began hurting.

"Billy is really cut up about it," Lucy told me, shaking her head.

"Billy?"

"Billy Schuyler," said Lucy, laughing at me, but getting irritated. I knew the symptoms well by now. "Kathleen's only been dating Billy for a year, Alison, seven nights a week. You can't pretend you haven't noticed *that*, Alison."

I could only stand there and gape at Lucy. My best friend from childhood had a boyfriend as steady as that, and I didn't even know who he was.

Lucy shrugged her eyebrows at me and kept smiling, the way you would at a spoiled brat you like in spite of his rotten behavior. "I . . . I'm busy," I said defensively. "My music is practically a full-time job, Lucy, what with having to memorize all those pieces and do all that practice. You just don't understand how much work is involved. I'll bet I've had to learn six or seven hundred pieces in the last year — and that's not exaggerating. Everything from Diana Ross and Eddie Rabbit and Bette Midler back to the Beatles back to the Kingston Trio back to *West Side Story* back to —"

"I get the point," said Lucy. "You don't have to brag all the time, Alison."

I choked back another defense. "When is the party?" I said.

"Saturday night," Lucy repeated.

I looked at my engagement calendar. I was playing the piano for a dinner party.

"Anybody would think you were the presidential aide for foreign affairs," said Lucy irritably. "Don't you ever move without that fat, foolish book?"

"I'm sorry," I said desperately. "I would if I could." She didn't want me to explain anything to her. She didn't care that I had made a commitment and had to stick to it. She just smiled at me tightly and moved on.

I felt as isolated from high school life as if Lucy had shut a door and bolted it.

How could I possibly go play some dumb piano pieces for some middle-aged clods when my best friend Kathleen's good-bye party was that night? How could I not have known Kathleen had a boyfriend? Or that she was moving?

I tried to picture Lucy's party. All my old friends sitting around in pajamas, giggling, telling scary stories and . . .

What is the matter with me? I thought. That's what we did in the sixth grade. Nobody is having slumber parties any more. This party will be . . .

. . . the kind of party where I usually sit on a piano bench. Where people drift up to the piano and ask for "our song."

Our song. I wondered if Kathleen and her Billy had an "our song." If they danced closer and looked at each other more lovingly when somebody like me played it.

One thing for sure. *I* didn't have a song, unless it was "Work, Work, Work."

I had one more class. I didn't spend it thinking about music but I didn't pay any attention to the teacher either. I sat there looking at the backs of people's heads. At boys' shoulders and girls' fluffy hair. At oxford collars and pullover sweaters. I settled on one particular back view: a senior boy who played football and whose shoulders consequently took up a lot more room than anybody else's.

Good grief, I thought. I'm behind in every class, I have a rough gig coming up, I've completely lost touch with every friend — and I'm sitting here rhapsodizing about *shoulders*.

The shoulders were very restless. They kept twitching and shifting, and twice fingers crept around awkwardly to scratch between them. I thought, if I were just one seat closer, I could scratch his back for him.

Just then he turned around. You know that awful moment when somebody you've been staring at catches you staring at him? You feel *guilty*, as if you've been cheating on a test or something, and you blush.

I thought, You really know you're at the bottom when you've been caught daydreaming about scratching somebody's shoulder blades. I comforted myself that at least I couldn't be any worse off. Things could only get better. I even toyed for a moment with the idea of skipping my gig to go to Lucy's party . . . but no, then things would get worse. Ralph would probably knife me or something.

27

Ralph. Now there was a male who spent plenty of time around me.

I considered the possibility of having a crush on Ralph. There were several drawbacks. First crushes should just spring themselves on you, not be carefully planned during English Literature. Second, Ralph was old. Third, I had just established that I was overdosing on music. If I hung around Ralph any more than I already did, I would drown in it.

So much for the only available man in my life.

I went back to studying shoulders.

4.

The problem in playing for people your parents' age is that you make them feel old, which depresses them. Then they wish you weren't there playing the piano after all, which rather dampens your performance. So for that Saturday's dinner party, without the combo there to look old for me, I had to look old on my own.

I wore concert black: a shimmering, black knit shirt, a six-chain necklace of rhinestones, and long rhinestone earrings. A matching tight black skirt studded with sparkles and streaked with black satin ribbon. I braided my hair into a complex arrangement with several tiny black satin bows.

And I was terrific. (One thing we musicians are is confident. At least, *I* call it confidence. My father says it's plain old conceit and I shouldn't be so proud of myself.) Still, I *was* terrific and the whole evening went wonderfully. I even got kissed by two guests — older than my father — who told me I'd been a joy.

Good jobs stay with you. I always feel kind of like a helium balloon after a good gig: floating and warm and up at the ceiling. Bit by bit you sag and get tired and come down.

I got home, said good night to Daddy, who always groggily waits up for me, and was hanging up my dazzling skirt when something punctured my balloon so fast I hurt inside.

The following Saturday night was another gig, but there was a message on my bed, in Daddy's handwriting, that it was cancelled; Ralph had phoned to say the club hadn't sold enough tickets. That meant I was free next Saturday night. Free to do what other girls might be doing on a Saturday night.

And that particular Saturday night was the Winter Dance. They would crown the Snow Queen (although we have yet to have snow on the ground the night of the Winter Dance). When I'd walked past the gym between classes yesterday, the decorations had arrived. Somebody's deparment-store-owner father had donated all the Christmas stars from his store: box after box of glittering, glistening, silvery-white stars to hang from the ceiling.

Everybody was going to the dance. Frannie, Lisa, Jan, Lucy, certainly Kathleen.

But not me.

Not Superwoman Brilliant Musician Conceited Booked-Up Alison.

On Saturday night I was going to be alone with nothing to do but maybe a few Algebra problems or a book report.

I stared at myself in the mirror.

The girl there looked rather elegant. Dramatic. Dark hair looped in intricate braids, her throat pale against a dark, soft neckline.

Nobody had asked that girl to the dance. Was it because any boy who knew Alison knew she would be busy? Or was it that no boy liked her enough to find out?

I stared at that Alison, and all of a sudden I wanted to peel her off. Scrub away the musician and the professional to find the plain, ordinary, high school girl who could relax and have fun and go out on dates.

And then I had the most horrible thought of all.

What if I gave up music only to find out that music was all I had? What if I quit the combo and backed off on all my jobs and had all the time in the world to spare and still nobody showed any interest in me?

I lay on the bed in the dark and told myself I would survive. All these troubles would build my character. Think how much character I would have by the time I got to college.

A few weeks later we played for the wedding of the decade (or so the newspapers called it). It was at Wind Gate Farms — the Fitzwilliam place. Fitzwilliam, as in ambassador to France, chairman of the board of I forget what conglomerate, and personal adviser to a former president of the United States.

Even Ralph said, "Wow."

Lizzie said, "Charge them a bundle."

I said, "Is the President coming?"

And Ralph said, "Guess what. There won't be a rehearsal."

At first I really didn't believe him. Bridal parties love to rehearse. They do it for hours, until everybody but them is going insane. "We'll have to wing it," said Ralph. "Everybody stay cool."

Wind Gate Farms sounded like a lot of cows in a pasture, but it wasn't. Deep in a woods of rhododendron and hemlock and tame deer, it was almost a castle. Lizzie said it deserved a gothic novel of its very own. I caught a glimpse of a magnificent garden, covered with snow, with only the complex outlines of its English boxwood hedges visible. The enclosed courtyard would easily park a dozen cars, but the butler (I kid you not) asked us to park our rather disreputable-looking van behind the barn. Barn, they called it. To me it looked like a mini-mansion. Inside, I'll have you know, were peacocks. In summer they normally strolled about the grounds.

Well, this is it, I thought. If I'm ever going to meet an exotic, romantic, exciting man, it'll be here.

I pictured a tall, lean, dark, senator's son. Or perhaps a blond, tanned, ambassador's nephew. I decided he'd be about twenty. A college junior. He'd seen me at the piano, hear my beautiful music, and he'd be so entranced he'd find himself crossing the crowded room to meet me. I'd make room for him on the bench. We'd sit very close and he'd whisper in my ear.

Lisa, Jan, and Frannie would have been proud of me. Music was definitely not foremost in mind right then. I was too busy keeping a lookout for unattached, exotic young men.

32

We followed the butler down a vast hall ("Gallery," the butler corrected me) into a marvelous, enormous room with statues in curved niches, a marble floor, and a few hundred metal folding chairs that must have been taken from some church basement somewhere. "Tacky," Lizzie told the butler, and I cringed, but the butler just laughed and agreed.

I spotted two ushers right away. They were perfect: handsome, dark, lean, interesting-looking — and old. They looked practically as old as my father. "Phooey," I said gloomily.

"How many guests will there be?" said Lizzie to the butler.

"Two hundred for the ceremony. Six hundred for the reception."

Six hundred intimate friends, I thought. Who am I going to invite when I get married? I don't even have *one* intimate friend!

The wedding photographer, wearing a white turtleneck and vivid red plaid trousers, was leaping about like a jack-in-the-box getting good flicks of the flowers. Lizzie and I skirted the makeshift altar, which turned out to be empty cardboard liquor boxes stacked up and draped with white velvet! "Tacky," Lizzie and I said at the same time, and we giggled. "Look," she said, "there's another photographer. Doesn't he look newspaper-y? I have never been to a wedding that's been covered by a reporter. Maybe the president *is* coming."

This other photographer was a kid about my own age, wearing a camera and a baggy old suit, carrying a notebook and pens. I didn't think he looked newspaper-y. I thought he looked young.

He definitely did not look exotic.

I examined him carefully. He was rather good-looking, in a crinkly sort of way. He looked bored, as if weddings were not his favorite thing to report on.

Lizzie said, "You've been studying him for five solid minutes. What is it? Love at first sight?"

I blushed scarlet and sat right down to warm up at the piano. The piano, however, did not play. It clanked. It plopped. It banged. But it didn't play. "Ralph!" I howled.

"Mrs. Fitzwilliam!" Ralph howled.

A little horde of people quickly gathered around the piano: the wedding photographer, the newspaper-y kid, miscellaneous exotic ushers, and our combo. "Did you have the piano tuned?" said Ralph, which I thought was a rather stupid question.

"Tuned?" said Mrs. Fitzwilliam. "I had it polished. Isn't it a beautiful piano?"

We just sort of stood there. She left. Ralph said, "There's time to drive back to my place and grab my electric piano."

"No," said Lizzie, "you wouldn't get back in time. The rest of us will have to wing it."

I felt terrible. It wasn't my fault; it was the fault of the stupid, unmusical Fitzwilliams, but still, everyone except me was properly equipped.

"If you like," said the newspaper-y kid quietly, "I'll drive to your place and get your electric piano."

"You will?" cried Ralph. He tried to hug the boy, but the threat of a hug from Ralph tends to make people jump back.

"I'll go with him," I said. "I know the way. Give me your house keys, Ralph."

"Drive fast," said Ralph to the boy.

"No," said Lizzie, "the roads are icy."

"Don't listen to her," said Ralph. "The roads are fine."

The boy nodded at them both, giving the distinct impression that he could make his own decisions about ice and speed, and off we went.

The huge house was filled with people, milling about and embracing each other and drinking champagne. I could hardly keep up with the boy, hampered by my long skirt. He reached back, grabbed my hand, and hauled me along. Ah romance, I thought. My first walk down a corridor holding a boy's hand. I whipped around three people, whammed into another, and caught up to the boy so hard I slammed into him; and we both fell out of the mansion. "Sorry," I said.

"It's okay. I have plenty of vertebrae. I can spare a few."

We leaped over icy spots, dodged incoming guests, vaulted into his car, and drove out the back way.

"Belt up, will you?" said the boy impatiently.

I hadn't said a single word. I stared at him, flushing.

"Seat belt," he said, as if to a moron. "Put it on, will you?"

"Oh. Oh, right. Sure." I fumbled for the seat belt. It was a different model than the ones I was used to, and I couldn't get the silly thing to come out of its slot.

The boy sighed as if uncoordinated females

35

were always doing this sort of thing to him. Driving with one finger of his left hand, he leaned way over me, practically lying in my lap, and plugged me in. "We're going to get killed," I said indignantly. "Sit up and drive."

"We're driving over ice," he said. "You need a seat belt. My sister had an accident last month and got her face cut up because she didn't have her seat belt on."

"I know, but you were driving with one finger and not looking at the road in order to put it on me."

"It's a one-way road," he said, "and I was only down for a second."

After that we sat in a huffy silence.

Things are going fine, I thought. I broke his back when he tried to hold my hand and I'm scolding him about his driving technique when he's trying to get me a keyboard to play on. The way I handle boys, I should be ready for my first date when I'm, oh, say fifty-five.

"Turn left," I said. "Now down this little driveway. Bear right."

You can't beat *my* conversation, I thought. Light, funny, entertaining. "Stop. It's this one."

We struggled out of his car — struggled because I not only couldn't put the seat belt on, I couldn't get it off. Then we spent a full minute attacking the front door lock before deciding Ralph didn't have a key to his front door on his key ring. "This is like combat service," muttered the boy. The two of us staggered to the back door over Ralph's unshoveled path, where Ralph's deep boot holes had iced over, making solid snow sculptures.

My legs are not as long as Ralph's and his boot holes were too far apart for me. I could feel it coming like cruel fate. I was going to fall. I yelled, grabbed, twitched, and reached; and I fell anyway. Unfortunately, during a twitch I got hold of the boy's jacket and pulled him right over on top of me.

We lay there for a moment, and then he said, "What's your name?"

He sounded as if he kept a notebook full of the names of people he never wanted to see again and had a whole page waiting for me.

"Alison," I said.

He managed to flop over and get on all fours and crawl off me. "Funny," he said. "You didn't look this klutzy at the piano, Alison."

"I'm very coordinated at a piano. Really."

The way I got up out of Ralph's boot holes you wouldn't have thought I was capable of anything. I have never blushed so hard in my life. Even my elbows blushed. We got the back door open and walked gingerly into the kitchen. "Where is the piano?" said the boy grimly.

"You sound like a soldier who's regretting that he ever volunteered," I said.

"I'm tough," he told me. "I always finish a mission. No matter how many beautiful brunettes fling themselves on me. Now where is this portable piano?"

"It's under his bed. Ralph is sure somebody will break in here someday so he leaves the color television right out where they can't miss it, but his instruments he keeps under the bed."

We shoved piles of dirty socks and unplayed sheet music out of our way and hauled the keyboard case out from under the bed. It was an old model, not nearly as light and streamlined as they make them now. We each took a handle and lurched toward the door.

"This is portable?" grunted the boy.

"More so than a concert grand," I said.

The three of us did not fit through the kitchen door.

"You go on," said the boy. "We'll follow you this time."

It's pretty bad when a guy would rather have an electric instrument for company. I went out and concentrated very hard on where I put my feet.

We were backing out the driveway when I remembered I had forgotten to lock the kitchen door again.

"It's okay, Alison," he said. "There's nothing there to steal but the color TV now."

"Look out for that ice," I said.

"Thanks, I see it, Alison."

"Turn left here."

"Thanks. I remember the turn, Alison."

I thought, no wonder I have no boyfriends. I can't *talk*.

It seemed grossly unfair that he could call me Alison —he used my name as if it were a rock he was throwing at me — and I didn't have a name for him. I'll ask him his name, I thought. I'll say, What's your name? I rehearsed it mentally. I sounded like an army interrogation officer.

I could play Debussy and Chopin, Bacharach and Joplin. But I couldn't ask a boy his name. Stupid, stupid, stupid, I told myself. I said, "So. And what is *your* name?"

His profile was toward me. His cheek was wrinkled, as if bits of previous smiles were stuck to it. "Ted," he told me.

I had what I wanted. His name. And I couldn't think of one word to say to Ted now that I knew him. I like the laugh lines on your cheek, Ted. Thank you for not breaking my ribs when I made you fall on me. Tell me your last name. I want to telephone you. Ask me my last name. Ask me my phone number. Tell me you want to telephone me.

"We're here," said Ted. He didn't even mention my seat belt this time. He just reached over and unclicked it himself. What a nice arm you have, Ted, I thought. Pretty good fingers, too.

We vaulted out very athletically and after that staggered under the weight of the keyboard. Then we couldn't even get in the mansion, because our passage was blocked by loudly conversing, very jolly guests.

I said ineffectual things like "Excuse me, please?" "Uh, sir, could you move a speck to your left, please?" and nobody even noticed me, let alone moved.

In a big, barrellike voice, Ted informed the guests that it was time to shove over. "Musical instrument coming through," he yelled, and we used the keyboard as a battering ram. I wondered if some of the people we removed from our path were ambassadors, chairmen of boards, and advisers to presidents.

Ted and I rushed down the aisle, skirted the liquor-box altar, and set the keyboard down where Ralph was pointing. Ted plugged it in, I opened the legs and locked them, Ted slid a folding chair under me, and I joined in at the chorus without anybody missing a beat.

I was halfway through the "Wedding March" before I realized that I had not even thanked Ted for enduring all that for my sake.

5.

I love weddings. I love all those words about goodness and loyalty and love. I love the flowers and the vows and the misty eyes of grandmothers. This bride was perfect: small and slender with a delicate face half-hidden by swaths of cloudy veiling. Her groom was handsome and very nervous, and the minister had a fine, clear voice that made me shiver.

During the exchanging of rings, Ted squatted down next to me and began focusing his camera. I had almost forgotten that he was with a newspaper. I looked down into his hair, which was wavy and thick. His face was furrowed and he was concentrating very hard on his work. He didn't even know I was there. How well I knew the feeling!

Just as he was about to take the shot, the bridal party all suddenly shifted places and now the keyboard was in his way. Making a face and a little murmur that only I could hear, Ted got up off his knees and sat on my chair. The only trouble was,

I was taking up all the space. "Shove over," he hissed.

I gave him all but an inch.

He took about six photographs of the bride and groom exchanging vows, looking up into each other's eyes. I looked into Ted's eyes instead. It was difficult to tell what color they were and we were at very close range, too. Gray, I thought, from three inches away. Or bluish.

Ted had forgotten about me so completely that when he turned he was absolutely shocked to find another nose literally touching his. We sat there, squeezed on the folding chair, nose to nose, and all of a sudden it was funny.

The minister was leading a prayer.

The guests were absolutely silent.

And Ted and I were starting to giggle.

I took his elbow to help him contain his laughter. But laughs don't start in elbows; they start in chests, and I couldn't start hanging on his chest. It was the bridge and groom who were supposed to do the embracing, not the pianist and the photographer. I felt my own laugh spurting out of me and I practically crammed my fist down my throat to stop it. Ted took his pencil and wrote in big capital letters on a page of his notebook: GAG. Very quietly he ripped the word off and held it gently over my mouth.

I thought I would burst. My ribs hurt from holding in a laugh. And I wasn't even sure what was funny. If Ralph hadn't kicked me I would actually have missed my cue for the recessional.

We smashed into the march, all trumpet and drum and noise, and as the guests began talking and laughing, I said, "You know, Ted, it's rather difficult to play when I can't reach half the keyboard."

"Would you like me to mo— "

That was a tough question. I really did need access to the other half of the keyboard. On the other hand, no, I didn't want Ted to move. I liked him pressed up against me like that.

Ralph said, "Uh, kid, do you mind getting off Alison's chair? I would like her to contribute to this number, please."

Ted got up quickly and I shifted over. The seat was warm where he had sat. I hoped he would stay and talk to me but he didn't. He moved on behind me. I twisted once to see him but it wasn't possible. All I could see was the occasional flash of camera in the crowd.

We wrapped up the march, and I sagged with relief. I had not enjoyed that one. If I had really burst out laughing in the middle of somebody else's wedding . . .

What I had enjoyed was Ted. I looked around for him, but my view was blocked by gray pants. I looked up, past the belt and the jacket, and there was Ted. I stood up. We weren't nose to nose. He was taller. "Good nose," he said.

"Yours isn't bad either."

We giggled then. "So you're a reporter?" I said. "Yup."

I was pretty sure you had to have a college degree in English or journalism to be a reporter, which meant Ted could not be younger than twenty-one or twenty-two. But he looked about seventeen to me. Perfect age, I thought. Perfect nose. What else could I ask for? "Where do you go to school?" I said carefully.

"Western High. How about you?"

"J.F.K. High." That meant we lived on opposite sides of the city, which has five high schools. "What paper are you with?" I asked him.

"*The Register.*"

"You're a full-fledged reporter?"

"Do I look half-fledged?"

I giggled again. "No. You —"

"Alison," said Ralph, "arrange your love life on your own time. We have to get into the other room for the reception." He took my arm to pull me away from Ted. Obviously he felt force would be needed.

"Wait a minute," said Ted. "How was Alison supposed to play in another room? Did they expect you to roll their terrible grand piano down there?"

Ralph shrugged. "They've got another piano. In perfect shape. We found out about it just after you two left."

Ted and I looked at each other. "Oh," we said.

"It's like that sometimes," said Ralph. "Come on, Alison." He dragged me away. It seemed to me I had a fantasy about being fought over by two men. This wasn't quite what I had in mind. The one wanted me for my music; the other didn't care because he was off immediately taking more photographs.

Musically, receptions are a bore. Nobody is listening to you anyway, and as long as you keep the rhythm and the melody going they think they've gotten their money's worth. I've done the repertoire so often I don't even have to think about it to get it right. This was nice, because I could use the reception time to daydream about Ted. It would have been a drag to have to pay attention to my music as well.

Ted drifted around the huge buffet, stuffing himself. It seemed unfair that he could eat and I had to sit there working. By the time the reception was over and I could stop playing, the food would be all gone. And these people had civilized food. Roast beef and cheese and cold salads mixed in with their nauseating fish eggs.

Ted materialized by my elbow. "You like petit fours?" he said.

"Love them."

He popped a chocolate-and-mint petit four into my mouth.

"Romance at the piano," said Ralph. "I'm too old for this sort of thing. Ted, old boy, bring me something, too. A whole plateful, if you don't mind. Lots of rolls. None of your romantic little cakes. I'm starved."

So Ted very obligingly filled up plates for everyone. Between melody lines Ralph would grab a quick bite. I had to play some very long tags so he could finish chewing. But I didn't mind. Since I couldn't eat with my fingers, Ted fed me.

I kept thinking that we would drive home together, Ted and I. We'd laugh about falling over and getting ice in our shoes. We'd talk about his being a reporter and my being a musician. We'd get nose to nose again, and maybe lip to lip.

Ted said, "I have to go. Got to get this to the paper by five. Nice meeting you, Alison. Take care of yourself."

And he was gone.

I was playing, "What the world needs now, is love, sweet love." I thought, Who cares about the world? Alison, I, Alison, need love, sweet love.

But Ted needed to get his pictures and his story in to his paper. I wondered what he had thought about me. Was I just a creature who had tripped him up, but nevertheless worth a few minutes' effort of food-stuffing? Did he think I was interesting? Or just an unbelievably hungry piano player?

"I never thanked him," said Ralph. "What was his name, Alison? I'll call him up tonight."

"Ted," I said. I thought what a nice secure easy name Ted was.

"Ted what?" said Ralph irritably.

I didn't know his last name. I'd forgotten to ask. "Maybe he'll have a by-line on his article," I said. "Buy *The Register* and see."

But when *The Register* came out, it had three photographs of important guests and three paragraphs of data about them . . . and no by-line.

I considered going over to Western High and standing in the central hall waiting for Ted to pass by. I could sort of flag him down. Hi, I'd say, I was just passing through.

He would probably suspect something.

"What I suspect," said my father, frowning at me, "is that you have gone and gotten a crush on somebody."

"You don't go get crushes," I told him. "Crushes come and get you."

Daddy nodded sagely. "That's the worst kind," he said.

And he was right. I had the worst kind. The biggest, heaviest, most ridiculous crush I could ever have imagined. On a boy whose last name I didn't even know. I would probably never run into Ted again.

I actually lay in bed thinking about his nose. It worried me that I wasn't sure what color his eyes were. How could I go on with this crush when his eyes might be gray or they might be blue?

Coming up that week was an Elks' Club Dance, the Women's Clubs Annual Combined Awards Dinner, and a thirtieth wedding anniversary. I doubted very much that Ted would be at any of those.

I bought every issue of *The Register* that week. I didn't read many of the articles, but I checked out all the by-lines. If they had a reporter whose first name was Ted, they weren't mentioning it.

He was a mirage, I thought. I've got a crush on a cloud.

6.

"Saw you the other day," said Mike MacBride. "All red ribbons and glitter going into the country club."

I nodded. That outfit has too many spangles for my taste. But as Ralph points out, the customer isn't paying all that money to watch a bunch of post office clerks at work. I have a long dark cape I wear over it during the winter, to sort of hide beneath.

"And that cape!" said Mike. "You looked like Superwoman, all right. Ready to swirl off and save the world."

Evidently the cape wasn't too good for camouflage. My cheeks went as red as the spangled costume. "It was just the Women's Clubs Annual Combined Awards Dinner," I said.

"Hey," said Mike, laughing. "Sounds exciting."

"No — stodgy." I smiled up at him. He was just about the same height as Ted. I could tell by the distance between our noses. And Mike's eyes were definitely brown, dark deep brown.

"You ought to rev things up with a little hard rock," said Mike.

"They don't want to notice anybody but themselves," I told him. "We're just background."

"Background?" said Mike. "In that red outfit? Not likely."

He was cornering me on the third floor and I had to get to gym in the basement. Ms. Santora had told me if I came in late one more time, she'd knock my grade down. I tried to decide whether a good gym grade was more important than small talk with Mike McBride.

If it had been Ted, there'd have been no question.

It was so ridiculous to be talking with a real, live, interested, handsome boy right there in the hall — just the daydream I'd always had — and be comparing him with a boy I didn't even know. "Could you walk down toward the girls' gym with me?" I said. "I'm really worried about being late again."

Mike hesitated. He's pretty large, as football players tend to be (successful ones, at least), and when Mike hesitated the whole corridor of passing students hesitated with him. "Okay," he said smiling, "fine. I guess I can be late to Trig instead of you being late to gym."

I actually argued with him. I told him that Trig was more important than gym, I shouldn't have asked him, he should go on to Trig.

"Pick up your feet, will you?" said Mike. "At least one of us should get to a class on time."

I picked up my feet. From the direction he was propelling me, I could tell that I was going to be

49

the one getting to class on time. I wished it could be summertime, when nobody had to go anywhere, and Mike and I could just wander around and talk. No, it had to be school — and gym, of all things — and we were going into a hall that smelled of old unwashed gymsuits and sweaty sneakers. If there is anything less romantic than that, I don't want to hear about it!

Mike, like Ralph and Ted, had very long legs. I had to trot beside him. I thought how terrible it would be if I fell over with Mike the way I had with Ted. On the other hand, maybe it would lead to something interesting.

Mike was talking about a ball game. I had been paying a lot of attention to Mike, but absolutely no attention to what Mike was saying. I hadn't any idea whether he'd been in the game, or seen the game, or read about it in the sports pages. I didn't even know what sort of ball was involved. Surely not football, this time of year. "Mmmmm," I said, trying to sound understanding and interesting.

Mike gave me a peculiar look. "Who was the guy whose van you got out of at the country club?" he said.

"Ralph. He runs the combo."

"Ralph ever get substitutes for you?"

"Oh, sure." I told him about my father's rules on wild parties.

"How awful," said Mike. "You go to all the dreary, boring, middle-aged stuff and you have to stay home for all the good ones."

"Right," I said. I thought, wow, Daddy wouldn't like Mike. Daddy doesn't think the wild parties are the good ones. I looked up at Mike again and wondered if all the parties Mike went to were wild. I had a feeling they would be.

Ted. Somehow I didn't even picture Ted at parties. I pictured him doing things alone. Doing interesting things. Skydiving, maybe, or hiking the entire Appalachian Trail.

"So if you ever really wanted not to work some night," said Mike, "Ralph isn't necessarily dependent on you."

"Right. The world is full of keyboard men."

"You are not," said Mike McBride, looking down at me and taking my arm as we got to the top of the next flight of stairs, "definitely not, a keyboard *man*."

I flushed. All I could think of was falling. He was going to spring compliments on me and, I was going to tumble down a flight of stairs like a complete klutz. I hung on to his hand on one side and the railing on the other, like a cripple. The distinctive odor of the locker rooms wafted up to meet us.

"I hardly ever come down here," said Mike. "Feels like alien territory."

"Feels alien to me, too," I told him. "I hate gym. The only reason I'm even passing Physical Education is because I do attend. They can't flunk you as long as your body is on the floor."

Mike frowned. "You don't like gym?" he said. "But you like sports, don't you?"

Too late I remembered that sports were the center of Mike's life the way music was the center of mine. "Sports," I said feebly, trying to think of one.

Mike just laughed. "Nice to talk to you, Alison," he said. "See you around." His thick sneakers pounded on the stairs going back up.

Stupid. The adjective belonged to me. Mike had all but said that he liked me, and he wanted to know if Ralph ever gave me free evenings. I told myself Mike had rushed away to get to Trig, but I really knew he had lost interest in me. How could I blame him?

I changed into my nasty gym clothes (I admit to being partially responsible for that ripe odor in the halls) and went out into the gymnasium. We were doing gymnastics. Or rather, other people were doing gymnastics. I was standing around wondering how they could bend their bodies like that.

"Alison," said Ms. Santora helplessly, "you're so slim and trim and you must be well coordinated or you couldn't play the piano. But you can't even find the mat, let alone tumble on it."

"Actually," I said, "falling is one of the things I do best."

I tried to do a somersault, fell heavily on my side, and struck the tumbler next to me with my left foot. For the millionth time, I thanked God that gym is not coed. If I have to make a fool of myself three times a week, at least I don't have to do it in front of the boys.

Boys, I thought.

I narrowed that down quickly. Boy. Ted. Two very fine three-letter words.

It was much easier to daydream about Ted, whom I didn't and wouldn't know, than about Mike, who was real and there and required effort I didn't know how to make.

7.

"You know, honey," said my father at supper, "I always thought you'd be a companion to me in my old age. But I'm hardly even middle-aged yet, and you're off seven nights a week gallivanting."

"I'm not gallivanting, Daddy, I'm working."

We were having frozen pizza. We both hate cooking. Hate it. We eat a lot of frozen dinners, tons of junky fast food, and consider it the height of domesticity when we scramble eggs and make toast. The way we eat is boring, expensive, and probably not very nutritious, but it suits us.

"Sometimes I worry about what your mother would say," my father told me. He finished his pizza and began tugging at his hair, which is a sign that he's about to deliver a distress lecture. I'm not sure he even knows what Mother would say about that. They had known each other only two months when they got married; I was born eleven months later, and she died six months after that.

This time Daddy was sufficiently upset to get her photograph off the piano. We have a nice old

Yamaha grand, and Daddy likes to keep their wedding picture propped up on it. Every single time I practice I have to set it on the floor so it won't fall off and break during the banging of chords. It's dreadful to think that my only contact with my mother is impatiently moving her wedding picture out of my way.

"Your mother would want you to have a more normal social schedule, honey," said my father.

"I'll second that," I said.

My father nearly dropped his napkin. "You would?"

"I'm normal, Daddy. I'd like to date. Have boyfriends."

"Then why don't you?" He was honestly puzzled. You would have thought I could run downtown and buy a boyfriend at the department store. Pick my size, keep my change, and live happily ever after.

I shrugged and shoved the pizza leftovers into their cardboard box.

"Whatever happened to that Ted you were mooning over?" he asked.

"I was not mooning over him. And I don't think anything happened to Ted. I've just never run into him again." I tried to be very offhand about Ted.

"Why don't you call him up?" said Daddy. "Ask him out. This is a new world, you know. Equality between the sexes and so forth."

The mere thought of asking a boy out made me queasy. Fortunately, I had a very logical answer for Daddy. I didn't know Ted's name and consequently could not look up his phone number.

Daddy picked up the photograph of Mother. "She's beautiful," he said. "You look just like her."

I stared at the face, frozen there for all these years, the only face I knew for her. I didn't know my mother angry or laughing or tired or proud. I only knew her calm and waiting for the photographer to snap the picture. I wondered if she had been well organized. If she could have fit school and a music career into one life. I was organized down to the last tube of toothpaste, and I was still missing out on half of what was out there.

The male half, among other halves.

I decided to go over to the Devaneys and say good-bye to Kathleen decently, not just shout it at her during changing periods at school.

"Alison!" cried Mrs. Devaney. She hugged me fiercely. "It's been so long. Come in, darling. Kathleen tells us all the time about your music. We're all so proud of you."

Now *there* was a welcome!

I followed her into the den, and sitting around on couches, in chairs, and on the floor, were the three Devaney girls and their three boyfriends. I don't think I have ever in my life felt so lonely as I did at that moment, being introduced to three hugging couples. I'd played jump rope and horses and Spud with the Devaneys, Bridget had taught Kathleen and me how to put on mascara, and Annie was the first kid I ever baby-sat for.

And now they all sat with their hands entwined with boys I'd never met. I was the only person in the room without a partner.

Mr. Devaney started things off wonderfully by asking why I hadn't brought my boyfriend along.

I managed to laugh. "I don't have one to bring," I said.

"Ah," said Mr. Devaney. "Between men, huh? Beautiful girl like you." He shook his head sadly and began describing the social lives of his three daughters. Bridget, Kathleen, and even thirteen-year-old Annie had obviously dedicated themselves to the pursuit of men. It sounded like fun.

Kathleen said, "Dad, Alison doesn't want to hear all that now. You hush for a moment and let us talk."

"Tell her about the wedding," said Mr. Devaney.

"The wedding!" I gasped. I stared at Kathleen and at Billy. Getting married at sixteen? Surely she wasn't really going to do that! It would be crazy!

The Devaneys shrieked with laughter. "Bridget," they told me. "As soon as she graduates from college this June."

"Oh." I felt totally stupid. The entire evening was just the same. I didn't know the Devaneys anymore; I couldn't share their jokes; I didn't feel like a part of their family.

I felt terribly, totally lonely.

Kathleen kissed me good-bye on the cheek; her boyfriend shook hands with me. We agreed that it had been nice, and I went on home.

Annie, I thought. Even little Annie can rack up boyfriends.

I walked heavily in the door. The phone was ringing. I didn't feel like answering it. It would only be Ralph.

On the sixth ring I gave up and answered. It was Ralph. I sighed.

"That kid Ted who drove you to get my electric piano," said Ralph.

"Yes? What about him?" My heart leaped about seven stories up from the cellar where it had been at the Devaneys.

"You remember him?"

"Yes," I said distinctly. "I remember Ted."

"He called me."

"He called *you*?" I said. It seemed to me if Ted were going to make a phone call, he should at least make it to me.

"Yeah. He wanted your phone number. I gave it to him and he gave me his to give to you in case he doesn't reach you so you can call him. That make sense?"

I didn't think it made a whole lot of sense, no, but it certainly made me happy. "What's his last name, anyhow?" I said. "Did he tell you his last name yet?"

"I didn't ask and he didn't say."

Terrific. If we did have a date I would have to pick his pockets, sneak a look in his wallet, read his driver's license, and *then* I'd know Ted's last name.

"I know," said Ralph brightly. "You've got his phone number. Go through the entire phone book, number by number, until you —"

I hung up on Ralph.

8.

First I waited three minutes to see if the phone would ring and it would be Ted. Then I panicked. I would have to call him.

He loves me, I thought, mentally stripping a daisy of its petals. He loves me not. He needs a pianist for his birthday party to which he will ask some other girl. He wants to ask *me* to a party. He needs to know the name of a Baroque composer for a history exam and figures I'll know. He wants my company. He cracked a rib falling down and wants to sue me.

Eight-six-nine, six-one-seven-eight.

It was a pretty catchy number. I might set it to music. Setting it to music would definitely be less traumatic than dialing it.

I eyed the telephone. Previously it had been a small white object with a gentle bell. Now it was The Enemy.

The more I thought about telephoning Ted, the more I thought it was a miracle that anybody ever got asked out on any dates at all — considering the courage it takes to dial a number and ask a question.

I remembered the shape of Ted's nose and the way he had fed me petit fours. Love, I told myself. He wants to get to know me better. I picked up the receiver and dialed eight-six-nine, six-one . . .

Ralph, I thought. Mean, sinister, untrustworthy Ralph. I bet this is a practical joke of his. Ted didn't call him at all. When I phone that number it's going to be a pizza house or one of Ralph's extra drummers.

I picked up the phone book this time. Ours is about two inches thick, excluding yellow pages. I did not really want to work my way through it one number at a time to locate and verify the number.

Strength, I told myself. Backbone. Character. This is where we separate the sheep from the goats.

Eight-six-nine, six-one . . .

I put the phone back down. If Ted planned to ask me out, I needed my datebook right there so I could see when I was free. I got the engagement calendar out of my purse and studied it. I was pretty heavily booked up but, frankly, there wasn't one commitment in there I wasn't willing to sacrifice. Ralph probably wouldn't feel that way, but I wasn't his slave. He could find another keyboard man.

I waited another fifteen minutes for Ted to call me, but the phone didn't ring.

Then I spent fifteen minutes planning what I would say if all Ted wanted was a pianist and not a date.

By that time it was too late for anybody to

telephone anybody and I had to go to bed. I lay there meditating on two things. One, was Ralph really sufficiently cruel to play a joke like this? Two, what color *were* Ted's eyes?

Around one o'clock in the morning I remembered that I really should be thinking about an English Lit essay test, but somehow Ted's eyes were more interesting.

By morning I knew I was being very childish and silly about the whole thing. The only way to resolve this was simply to dial the number and see who answered. I waited until my father was in the shower so he couldn't listen in.

Eight-six-nine, six-one-seven-eight.

There was no answer. I was very sure because I let it ring seventeen times. Afterwards, I wondered what I would have done if someone had picked it up on the seventeenth ring and demanded to know what kind of worthless, interfering person would let a phone ring seventeen times when other people were trying to sleep late.

I went off to school to take my English Lit essay test, and all through the test I was sort of humming to myself: eight-six-nine, six-one-seven-eight.

"I knew you were peculiar," said Frannie at lunch, "but singing happily through that terrible Lit test? Honestly, Alison, if I'd had a china plate I'd have broken it over your head."

"I'm sorry," I said humbly. "I didn't know I was doing it out loud."

"What was the song, anyway?" said Lisa. "I didn't recognise it."

I blushed scarlet. "Can't remember," I mumbled, and cleared my place quickly and left early for my next class. I had to go through the main hall to get there. There's a pay phone in the hall. It attracted me enormously. Silly dope, I told myself, Ted's in school right now, too.

I wafted through the rest of the day. I had convinced myself that Ted also had a crush on me, that it really was his number, and that we were destined for a long and loving relationship.

After school I decided against using the pay phone because the lobby was crammed with people, all of whom lean against the pay phone and make wisecracks whenever it's being used. I went on home and there was my father, having a snack — a large one — that would take him half an hour to eat, what with the paper there for him to read . . . right next to the phone.

Ted didn't call me. My father didn't leave his post. We went out for supper and Daddy dropped me off at Rob's junior high, where he teaches band and where our combo has its rehearsals. I walked in warily waiting for Ralph to make some snide remark, but the only snide remark Ralph made was about how I didn't modulate very well from E flat to G and what kind of musician was I anyway?

It didn't bother me at all. If Ralph didn't hassle me over Ted, then it really was Ted's number he'd given me and not some joke. I went straight home after rehearsal and it was only eight forty-five, so I dialed the number.

"Ted?" said a tired, irritated voice. I couldn't even tell if it was a male or female talking to me.

"Yes, please," I said.

"Ted left half an hour ago. He won't be back until late."

"Oh," I said.

"You want to leave a message?"

I tried to think of an intelligent, noncommital message to leave.

"You from the paper?" said the voice.

"No. My name is Alison Holland and Ted asked me to call him."

The voice coughed a few times, cleared its throat, yawned, and finally said in a much more pleasant, female tone, "Okay, I wrote that down. And who are you, please? Did he interview you?"

"No, ma'am. I'm a musician he met a few weeks ago."

The voice climbed an octave, getting edgy and suspicious. "Musician?" said the woman. Obviously, to her musicians were drug-popping, orgy-organizing fiends. I tried to sound very innocent and ordinary. "Could you just tell Ted I returned his call? My number is —"

"I'll tell him," she said, and hung up.

At least it gave me something new to worry about all night. It was probably Ted's mother. She would probably not give him the message because she didn't like musicians, and in the meantime Ted would have met some super girl and forgotten me.

Several things happened over the rest of the week. We had two important gigs, I earned a lot of money, Daddy changed jobs, I aced the Lit test and got D-plus on a surprise Latin quiz, war broke out all over Central America, and new cancer-causing agents were discovered.

I, however, was concerned solely with a little white telephone that did not ring when I watched it.

On Wednesday my father said, "Oh, I forgot to tell you that some boy called."

I froze. He did not elaborate. "And?" I said.

"And I said you weren't home."

Now I knew what teachers meant when they said that getting answers was like pulling elephants' teeth. "And what did he say?"

"He said he'd try again."

"Who was it?"

"He didn't say."

I revved up my courage and dialed eight-six-nine, six-one-seven-eight again.

"Yes, Alison," said Ted's mother, "he tried to call you back, too. I'm afraid he isn't here right now. The newspaper called and he's covering a United Fund Drive meeting."

That sounded just about as interesting as our gig for the Annual Club Women's Combined Award Dinner, or whatever it had been. At least I hadn't had to *write* about that. I wondered how Ted could stand all that stuff. He'd actually have to pay attention to what was being said.

Once I got into the swing of dialing that number, it got easier and easier. I almost forgot why I was calling Ted; it was just a habit I got into. I finally reached him before breakfast, an hour his mother suggested when she grew tired of exchanging remarks with me twice a day.

"Oh, hi," said Ted, yawning hugely into his end

of the phone. I visualized him half-awake. Half-dressed.

"Hi," I said. "I got your message to call you."

And then I felt stupid. Stupid right down to the smallest capillary and the least significant cell. I had made no fewer than eleven phone calls to try to reach this kid. Talk about excessive eagerness. His whole family was probably joking about it right now. "Hey, Ted," they'd say, laughing hysterically between bites of toast, "it's that crazy girl again."

"Lemme wake up," said Ted groggily. "Sorry, but I'm not at my best at six-thirty." There was a slurping noise and Ted said, "There. Okay."

"What was that?"

"My mother just gave me a cup of coffee. Now that my tongue is burned we can talk."

And talk Ted did. About his paper. *The Register.* The wonderful, interesting, meaningful *Register.* About how on Sundays they had a section of the paper devoted to people in the community who were of special interest to the readership. About how the editor of that section had agreed that a successful teenage girl band musician would be a very interesting article.

"Crush" is a funny word. My crush on Ted vanished within moments. It was replaced by humiliation and depression and disappointment, and I want to tell you that that was just as crushing. Worse, maybe. Even my tongue felt weighted down. I hoisted it up and said politely that I would think about it.

"How about today?" said Ted. He sounded very eager and anxious. I tried to feel flattered but that hurt even more. What he was anxious about wasn't me — it was the article he planned to write and the photographs he planned to take.

"I don't think so," I told him. "I have a rehearsal after school with a wedding soloist and —"

"That would be perfect!" Ted cried. "I could photograph you in action. Let me come to the rehearsal, please?"

That didn't exactly thrill me. Here I had been up nights planning all these lovely dates of dancing, movies, skating, walking, kissing, hugging — and I was going to end up on a piano bench again with a flash bulb going off in my face. "It's okay, I guess," I said. "But the soloist might object."

"I won't photograph her. It won't bother her at all. What time is the rehearsal and where?"

As I told him, I pictured his engagement calendar. It would be just like mine. Fat and scribbled on. He'd have a pencil in his hand. He'd be the sort whose pencils were always sharp and whose pens were never out of ink.

I said good-bye.

All day in school I caught myself fantasizing that at *this* meeting Ted would get to know the real Alison and be so taken with her that he would ask her on a real date. I tried to stop myself. I was never going to have a real date, because the only date anybody ever wanted Alison Holland for was a paying club date.

9.

I walked into the church, Ted carrying my
music and my organ shoes, as if he really were my
boyfriend and was coming along for the pleasure
of my company. It felt sort of comfortable to have
him walking along next to me. I had the sensation
that he and I had done this many times and would
do it many more. It was a warm feeling, but when
I looked over at him to see if he shared it, Ted
was staring at the stained glass windows and
wondered how old they were. "Centuries," I said
grumpily and stalked up to the organ.

Whoever had told the soloist she could sing
should be imprisoned. The rehearsal was awful. It
made my stomach twist to think of her actually
singing out loud at a wedding. The only good
thing was that she demanded to know who Ted
was and he told her! "I'm Ted Mollison, ma'am,"
he said. He had a deep, nice voice. I decided to
overlook his interest in the stained glass windows
and enjoy our interview. Or at least enjoy his
voice during it, even if he behaved like a turkey by

being completely professional and not at all interested in me personally.

Mollison, I thought throughout the rehearsal. He's Molly's son. I wondered if that stern-sounding woman on the phone could really have a name as warm and friendly as Molly. No. She probably had a name like Prudence or Hildegarde.

Ted Mollison. It had a nice sound.

Nicer by far than the sounds the soloist was making.

"Whew!" said Ted, when the soloist had finally given up and left us. "They pay her to sing?"

I laughed, glad to know that Ted could at least distinguish between a horrible voice and a decent one. "I doubt it. She's probably somebody's favorite aunt."

"She won't be such a favorite after the wedding, I bet," said Ted. He turned off the church lights before I was ready and I fumbled in the dark, trying to gather my music together. "I'll help," said Ted, but he didn't help by turning on the lights — he helped by bending over to pick up my music with me.

We crashed skulls.

Other girls, I am confident, would manage to touch fingertips. I, Alison had to crash into him with my rock-hard cranium.

The church was filled with gentle groans as Ted and I simultaneously dropped whatever music we had picked up and clutched our heads. I staggered past him and found the light switches again. We eyed each other rather bleakly. He's going to figure I'm so dangerous he can't be around me, I thought. If I'm not plotting how to break his ribs,

I'm trying to give him a concussion. I'm worse than being on the football team.

"I'm sorry," I said.

Ted held up a hand to stop me from bending down again to get the music. "One of us at a time," he said firmly. When he was very sure his upturned palm had stopped me from getting closer to him, he bent over and retrieved all my music. Stacking it very neatly and carefully, he said politely, "We ready to go now?"

But we weren't. I had to change my shoes. I had never felt so stupid. I had to sit on the chancel steps, untie the laces of my organ shoes, put those shoes back in their box, and jam my feet into my old sneakers. I was so upset with myself I could hardly tie the dumb things. Ted watched me with a sort of awed appreciation for anyone so uncoordinated that she couldn't even tie a bow on her sneakers.

I waited for him to make some sort of snide remark like did I require assistance in getting dressed each morning, but he didn't. He just gave me a rather determined smile. I could just hear his mother Hildegarde telling him if you're going to have to do something anyway, best to do it with a cheerful smile. Mother's well-trained boy Ted gave me a glued-on, cheerful smile.

We climbed into Ted's car. After I accidentally distributed his neatly stacked pile of my music all over the floor of the front seat, and after we had fished my Bach out from under his gas pedal, and after he had helped me figure out all over again how to fix his crazy seat belt, I was definitely ready for an early death.

Here I had spent my whole silly life learning

how to impress people with all my super skills, and the one boy I wanted to impress . . . you'd have thought my body consisted of old Jell-O.

"Well, I think I've got enough photographs," said Ted brightly. "All we need now is a place to talk. You want to go to the Burger Chef or Howard Johnson's on the turnpike and sit in a booth?"

I had no money on me. This wasn't exactly a date, and I had no idea if Ted planned to pay. I'd been so hard on him already — literally — that I didn't feel up to asking what the financial arrangements were on this. I rubbed my skull where it still ached from whacking his.

Ted, no doubt, was regretting he had ever gotten started on this interview. He was probably thinking it was truly miraculous that a girl could be a musician and still be a completely uncoordinated jerk. He had probably fastened my seat belt so that he wouldn't have to worry about me writhing all over the seat every time he made a left turn.

The more I looked at Ted, the cuter I thought he was. Sort of solid-looking. Friendly. The sort of guy you could snuggle up to and tell your troubles to and move on from those to . . .

"Don't worry," said Ted, "the newspaper pays for it. We can go anywhere and it won't cost either of us a cent." He beamed at me. Clearly the only decent thing about our whole afternoon together was that he didn't have to pay for it. "Okay," I said wearily, "then let's go to Howard Johnson's."

I was starving. Daddy and I eat at Burger Chef all the time. I might as well calm my growling stomach and my aching head with a new menu.

"I'd take you to my house," said Ted, "except that there's never any food there. We all work and nobody ever gets around to doing a big grocery shopping, so we never have more than enough food for the very next meal. If a war ever comes, we'll be the ones who starve first because all we'll have in the house is a bar of soap and a jar of pickles."

I burst out laughing. A boy with a mixed-up household just like mine. Well . . . no, really, not at all like mine. Starving is probably my father's greatest fear. Our house is stuffed beyond belief with canned ravioli and frozen waffles. "I'll pass on your house then," I told him.

And spent the rest of the drive scolding myself for saying that. Ted might think I meant I'd skip *him*, not his jar of pickles.

When we got to HoJo's, I shoveled my stuff out of my lap and tried to plan how to remove myself from the seat belt without falling on the pavement. Ted walked around the car to open the door for me. "Leave all your garbage there," he said, properly identifying my belongings. "I'll lock the car."

Just in case I was flattered that he was worried about my possessions, he added, "After all, my camera is in there."

Ted helped me out of the car. Now I don't normally require help anywhere and even if I did, nobody has ever offered it. Can you imagine Ralph asking me if he could open the door for me? Unless the door smashed my fingers, thus making it impossible for me to play our next gig, Ralph couldn't care less how I got through doors.

But Ted took my arm, extricated me from his seat belt, positioned my shoulder bag again on my shoulder, and turned me very gently away from the car. I was all set to feel warm and good about his attention — when I figured out the only reason he did all that was that he was afraid I might slam the door on the seat belt, and he wanted to feed it back into its slot. He did that. Lovingly. I wanted to make a smart remark about men who stroked seat belts for fun, but I had wrecked enough already. I kept silent.

After he'd locked up the car, Ted took my arm again, and we walked into the restaurant together. We took a booth in the corner and I sat opposite him. I watched his face. First he surveyed the restaurant, found that it looked exactly like every single other HoJo's on earth, decided that the other patrons didn't look all that interesting, and finally his eyes came to rest on me.

And he grinned.

Gosh, if I had been like old Jell-O before . . .

I thought that Ted Mollison had possibly the world's nicest smile.

This is an interview, I said to myself. *The Register* is paying for this and it is not a date. I will not see Ted again. I must be calm and professional as befits an interviewee. I must be fascinating and intriguing, however, so that Ted calls me up for a date anyway.

I tried to think of one single solitary fascinating thing to tell Ted about me.

The waitress, chewing more gum than any three people normally could, wanted to know what I was having. "Uh," I said, fascinating nobody.

Ted, the infuriating creature, was fascinated by the amount of gum in the waitress's mouth.

I gave up. Fascination was not my strong point. I didn't have any strong points except playing hit tunes. If I did have any, why, I'd already have a boyfriend.

"Could we see a menu, please?" said Ted.

The waitress mumbled something and ambled off. I figured she wouldn't be back for ten minutes. How was I going to be fascinating for ten whole minutes?

It turned out that I was not going to have time to worry about that. I was not even going to have time to read the menu. Ted shot questions at me like machine-gun bullets. He'd start with one topic and jerk into another and back to the first and off on a third. I could hardly keep track of anything and pretty soon I was just spouting answers without thinking — probably what Ted wanted. I wasn't sure it was what I wanted, though. I like to think long and hard before I speak.

He wrote it all down, too, in a shorthand notebook.

"Tell me the most embarrassing thing that ever happened to you."

I told the waitress I would have the seafood platter and told Ted about the Polish wedding where they had to explain to me what a polka was.

"Tell me about Ralph," demanded Ted.

I told him about Ralph. How come he didn't want to hear about Alison? Who cared about music and Ralph and gigs? I wanted to talk about me, and then I wanted to talk about Ted and me.

The delivery of our food was a welcome diversion for me, but Ted was just annoyed by it. He couldn't talk as well with his mouth full, and he was very impatient because I had to finish each mouthful before I could answer him. It is very hard to chew normally when the person across the table from you is tapping his pencil waiting for that chewing nonsense to finish up.

Finally Ted began talking about himself in order to fill the moments when I was chewing. I relaxed a bit and enjoyed my supper after all.

"Once," said Ted, "I interviewed this fascinating guy who runs the only one of this business in the entire world. He manufactures autographed baseballs."

I cracked up laughing. Imagine doing something like that all day every day of your entire life — writing names on little white balls. Ted laughed, too. "That's what I thought, but it turned out to be a fascinating business, especially if you like sports, which I do. Well, I not only sold my story to *The Register*, but I wrote it up differently — they call it *slant* in publishing jargon — and sold it to four major national magazines, including *Sports Illustrated!* Talk about a hit, Alison. There I was, sixteen, and I'd broken into four big, slick, tough, adult markets."

"Congratulations," I said, and I didn't say it lightly. I could well imagine how good the writing must have been to accomplish that. As Ted leaned forward, eager to tell the rest of his story, his notebook slipped and I saw that he had not been writing my words down in longhand, but in short-hand. He must have learned it because he felt he needed it for his career.

It was partly his story and what it had in common with my own, and partly his calling me Alison as if we were friends, not reporter and interviewee. Suddenly, overwhelmingly, I felt a deep kinship with Ted Mollison. I set down my fork and had a tremendous impulse to use that free hand to reach over and grab Ted's and say, "Ted, I feel a deep kinship with you."

The mere thought of actually doing that made me choke up with horrified laughter. How disgusted with me he would be then! The girl not only tried to break his bones, she got all soppy and maudlin on him.

"There wasn't one adult reporter on the whole *Register* who'd sold more than one article to a major magazine and most of them hadn't done that. Boy, was I cocky. I bragged until the staff was ready to slit my precocious little throat."

I could identify with that, as one who had done a lot of bragging in her time.

"But I never did it again, you see," said Ted, and there was a funny tired look in his face. "Since then I've never sold a single line to any publisher except *The Register*. I guess I've written fifty stories now that I thought were worth pub-lishing, and all I have is a box full of rejection slips."

Ralph handled all our bookings. I suppose that our combo had had its share of rejections. But I hadn't had to face the agony of being informed I wasn't worth anything. Ralph yelled at me from

74

time to time. I flubbed things now and then. But I was never thoroughly and completely rejected.

"I know how it must hurt," I said helplessly. I wanted to hug Ted. I wanted to say that *I* knew he wrote super stories even if the national magazines didn't.

Then I thought, I've gone crazy. I've never read one line by Ted Mollison. For all I know, he's illiterate and the editor at *The Register* spends every morning correcting Ted's stories. For all I know Ted's mother actually wrote the article about the autographed baseballs.

Ted cleared his throat, wrapping up that little moment of confidence. He looked flushed and disgusted with himself for saying anything. I wanted so much to talk with Ted about failure and success and trying again and again, but I couldn't seem to find the words fast enough. Ted said, "Your combo ever plan to go on the road?"

"No. Ralph went on the road for a few years and he makes it sound awful. Seventeen airports in twenty-two days, rundown motels in dreary industrial cities."

"Hey, neat," said Ted, grinning, "when do we leave?"

The grin almost unwrapped me. I restrained myself from saying that I would go anywhere with him, even seventeen airports in twenty-two days. Instead I gave him this dumb smile to fill up the space.

"You like what you're doing?" said Ted softly. "You have any regrets?"

I want to share my thoughts with Ted the way I never had with anybody. The table was this terrible obstacle, keeping us apart, and I could use words and we would understand each other and it would be such a wonderful thing, to have a friend who understood.

But Ted was not really interested in my regrets and griefs. He was writing an article to go in a newspaper that every family I knew read every afternoon. Did I really want people to know how lonely I was and how much I missed a normal high school social life?

"None," I said.

Ted shook his head. "I admire you. I think's it's hard as hell to juggle high school and a job, especially when people think you're too young for it and that you're probably not really serious about it."

I felt split, shattered almost. The one person I had met my age who would understand . . . but if I explained anything, his fingers were wrapped around that pencil and he would publish my answers.

"I know what you mean," I said, and I kept the rest of our conversation meaningless.

10.

"We've got a new form of competition," said Ralph gloomily at our next practice session.

"What's that?"

"Music is out," he said.

According to my schedule, music was still exceedingly fashionable.

"Video games," explained Ralph sadly. "Electronic games. *Rentable* video and electronic games. That Harrison party — the big reunion I've done each year for six years now? This year they're not having live music. They're renting enough different video games for everybody to play all night long."

"Now, Ralph," said Lizzie. "It's just one casual party. The whole career isn't down the tubes just because the Harrisons are hiring electronic games instead of a combo."

"These things spread," said Ralph darkly, as if we were discussing an infectious disease.

"Yeah, well, meanwhile, we've got four club dates this weekend," said Lizzie, "so let's jam."

I was using the piano bench as a desk to scribble out the rough draft of a book report. *This utterly stupid collection of poorly written stories,* I began.

No doubt it would turn out that my teacher's sister had written them. I scrunched up the paper and began again. *The beautiful prose of* — "Four club dates?" I yelled. "I have only three written down!"

"Friday is our regular end-of-the-month dance sponsored by the Downtown Businessmen's Association," said Ralph.

"Check."

"Saturday afternoon, Farkis wedding reception."

"Check."

"Saturday evening, dance at the convention of dental supply jobbers."

"Check."

"Sunday afternoon, your solo appearance at the Camellia Festival at the mall."

"Aaaaaaaaahhh!!" I had completely forgotten that. My whole Sunday schedule wrecked. Now I would never get the book report done.

Ralph just yelled at me for not keeping better track of things. I thought of Ted. I wondered if he had ever botched up his plans and missed an interview or a deadline. I wondered what he would think if I called him up and said I had blown my weekend. Would we talk about it, would we share? Or would he just be completely mystified about why that Alison Holland creature was bothering him?

Sunset Mall had two hundred stores arranged in a two-story star around a huge, egg-shaped stage. The stage handles everything from antique car exhibits to kids' Halloween painting contests. I hate that stage. It has no rails or benches at the sides, so you always have the feeling you'll roll down the curved, eggy parts and splat in front of the stores.

The owner of an electronic organ store was loaning an instrument for the occasion. It had so many gadgets I felt as if I were assembling a color television instead of playing a keyboard.

"Got to make a few sales here," said the organ man to me severely. "You play what the folks like, right?"

"Right."

And then, of course, I could not think of one thing to play. Not a single solitary melody came into my tiny mind. I stared at the organ keys as if they belonged to a typewriter.

Here it comes, I thought grimly. My first complete public failure.

"How about 'Mighty like a Rose'?" said the organ salesman. "Or 'I Love a Rainy Night'?"

It was sleeting out and this was a camellia exhibit, but he was paying, so I began the thin, mournful chords of "Rose."

"Hey there! Alison!"

I glanced up, startled, and who should be in front of the organ but Mike MacBride, with a girl I didn't know, and Dick Fraccola with Frannie. "What are you doing at a flower show?" I said, laughing. Immediately I was okay: I had an audience. I found my stride and failure disappeared.

"We're just wandering around," said Frannie. "We didn't even know about the flowers." She waved a bored hand at the long rows of tables all around me displaying camellias. "We're just kill-ing half an hour till the movie opens."

Perhaps if I had been better company that time when Mike walked me down to gym, I'd be the one waiting with him now, I thought.

"Would you play 'Evergreen'?" said Mike.

I was so sick of that song I wished it had never been written. "It's beautiful, isn't it?" I said, just the way Ralph had taught me. "Sure, I'll play it next."

Mike's eyebrows arched wistfully, waiting for it. Somebody should write a song about those eyebrows, I thought.

I wondered if Ted had good eyebrows. I could picture his face and his fingers and his hair, but not his eyes and eyebrows. Can't judge a man by his eyebrows, I told myself.

But if I did, Mike certainly came off well.

For about ten minutes the Camellia Festival was like a dream: two marvelous, handsome boys ignoring their dates and staring at me with respect and pleasure as I played for them. (I just hoped they didn't lean so hard on this portable organ that we all slid off the egg.)

And then some overweight, middle-aged man with a mustache that needed trimming asked for a John Philip Sousa march. The organ salesman nodded at me; obviously he wanted this potential customer pleased. Who cared what a bunch of teenagers wanted? They didn't buy organs.

Unfortunately, I had never had occasion to play any Sousa marches. Or anybody else's marches. I added a long tag to the rock number I was doing to give myself time to think. I hated to admit ignorance. On the other hand, if I tried to play a march and failed, the whole mall would know I'd been defeated.

Most of all, Mike and Dick would know.

Memories of football game marching bands at halftime came to me. I could feel a scrap of Sousa melody — that part where the piccolo shrills over the tubas. "Sure," I said to the customer, taking my reputation into my fingers. I launched full volume into a piece I didn't know, throwing on extra brass and percussion until the swell of the instrument filled the entire mall. The customer began marching in place beside me.

I absolutely hate it when adults act like little kids. I get so embarrassed for them. But I was getting paid and I had to be part of it. I had no choice but to nod, grin, and make marching movements with my elbows so the man would feel good about his marching.

People turned, smiling, because everybody loves a march.

When I finished, I got a super round of applause. I was flushed with pleasure. Without Ralph and the rest to carry me through, I'd winged it — when one mistake would have boomed out in two hundred stores.

I turned to see Mike's expression, but he was no longer there.

I searched the camellia crowd for him. After a minute I spotted the four of them sauntering down one of the star-shaped wings to the Cookie Monster Shoppe. Frannie was pointing at the fat sugar cookies decorated like Muppets, and obviously Dick planned to buy her one.

They had left while I was still playing. They hadn't been impressed at all. More likely they had been bored.

My chest hurt and my eyes blurred over. "I have to take a break," I said to the organ man.

"Sure, honey. Listen, you're super. You're fantastic. How about you and me working out something permanent? Okay?"

The way I felt then, the only thing I wanted permanently was out of music.

The organ salesman was hopping with excitement. He was selling more organs in half an hour than he usually sold in a week. "Okay?" he said. "Want to? Okay?"

It's not okay, I thought. I don't want some old organ salesman to call me honey. I want . . .

But I didn't know what I wanted.

If I had been able to sort that out, I probably wouldn't be faced with this sort of thing. I wanted everything. Settling for pieces of my dreams hurt. I kept a smile glued to my face and threaded through the camellias. Where, in a brilliantly lit shopping mall, was I going to find a corner of darkness? I had to sit down somewhere and pull myself together.

". . . personally prefer Blood of China," said a blue-haired old lady.

". . . has a nice bouquet, though," said her antique companion.

". . . horrible racket is over. I detest loud music."

". . . head aches from listening to that girl slam around on that dreadful instrument."

Somehow I got off the egg, but my smile was not going to last much longer. If only Lizzie or

Ralph were along! They knew how to shrug off anything. You have to be tough in this business, Ralph had said over and over.

Who wanted to be tough?

I managed to find a fat pillar to lean on, and the spotlights did create a pool of dark behind it, but my clothing was so gaudy I had no hope of really being hidden. Oh, for a bedroom with a door that closed so I could sob for a few minutes before going back on the stage!

I didn't have enough self-control to keep the tears back.

I reminded myself fiercely that I'd ruin my makeup, I'd look terrible, I'd make a display of myself . . . but it didn't help.

Just as my face crumpled into tears, a flash camera went off in front of me.

11.

"Alison!" said Ted. "What's the matter? That's not the photograph I expected to get. You were wonderful up there. What on earth is wrong?"

I had been right about him. He was a comforting person. His crinkly features crinkled some more as he put an arm around me, and then I had my dark corner — between the pillar and Ted's chest.

Nobody there but me and Ted's camera.

I laughed through my tears.

"What's wrong?" he said again, gently.

"I'm not sure, Ted. I guess I'm just tired. Letting small things get to me." I shrugged. I couldn't explain it. Maybe if we'd had hours ahead of us I could have worked into it. But I had only ten minutes and then I'd have to play some more.

"I was taking photos of the winning camellias," he said, "and you looked so smashing I wanted to get you, too. What happened? That funny old dude who wanted the march upset you?"

"No. It was the people who were annoyed by the music. Who wanted me to shut up."

Ted was incensed. "Somebody told you to shut up?" he demanded. He looked around, as if surveying the crowd for the sort of worthless clod who would tell a musician to shut up.

"No, no. I was just reading between the lines. Some people I knew walked away during the piece. I think my playing bored them. It . . . well, it hurt my feelings." I tried to laugh it off. "Silly, huh? You'd think I'd have the hide of a rhinoceros by now."

"No," said Ted, running a finger across my cheek. "I wouldn't think that at all."

We stood there, together, and a whole new set of feelings and wishes tumbled through me, like clothes in a dryer, rushing and flapping and falling and tumbling. His finger brushed my skin only for a moment, and I wanted him to do it all afternoon.

At the same instant we sort of stepped back, half-embarrassed, pretending nothing had happened.

"It's just that sometimes you think you're doing fine," I told him, "and you find out you've ruined it all."

Ted leaned back against the pillar and smiled at me. I thought, who needs Mike MacBride's eyebrows? I'll take a smile like this.

"Once I had a chance to cover a big fire," he said. "You might remember it. The one at the furniture warehouse down on Fifth Street that was started by arson about a year ago?"

I remembered it. They had been afraid the whole block would go. I wished Ted would hold me instead of talk to me.

"That was before I had my driver's license and nobody in my family was home to drive me. I raced over to our neighbor's and pleaded and begged and made all sorts of foolish promises about raking his yard and fixing his roof, so he drove me to the fire and we got there while it was still blazing."

I wondered what a fire had to do with anything. Did Ted just like the sound of his own voice or was he just trying to fill up an awkward space or was he going to tell me something?

"If," said Ted, "I had remembered to put film in my camera, I'd have had some good photographs, too."

We hung on to each other, laughing.

For me it was a moment of complete relief. Ted *did* understand. He *was* the same kind of person I was. He tried hard and sometimes he lost. He knew pain and embarrassment. He cared about whatever was bothering me. He was willing to tell me a crazy story about himself so we'd have something to share.

Ted handed me an enormous Kleenex and I mopped up my cheeks. "You look lovely," he said. "Listen, how long can you break?"

"Five more minutes, I guess."

Five crumby minutes. What we needed right now was five *hours*. I pictured myself going to the organ man and telling him I couldn't finish up my obligations to him this afternoon because this neat boy and I wanted to do some sharing. Somehow I did not think that would do a lot for my musical reputation.

"How about a frozen yogurt?" said Ted.

It sounded repulsive to me. But I did not think

it would be good tactics to reject Ted's first offer. "I've never had one," I said cautiously.

He put an arm around me and began leading me toward the stairs. His arm was wonderfully warm and solid, and somehow it protected me completely from the bored and the headachy camellia patrons.

"You have missed out, lady," said Ted. "I love frozen yogurt. You know what I spend my income on? Cameras, film, developing, gas for my car — and frozen yogurt."

"I guess I know your priorities now," I said, laughing. It was easy to laugh with Ted. In fact, we seemed to make a good couple to laugh *at*, as well. I in my flashy scarlet number and Ted in an old army jacket and faded jeans over work boots. The princess and the farmhand, as it were.

"What are yours?" said Ted.

"Mostly I save my money for college."

"I am impressed!" said Ted. He actually stopped me mid-stride, took both my arms, and stared down at me to verify that I actually did that sort of thing with my money. "My parents opened a savings account for me," he said, nodding over and over again. "They put twenty-five dollars in it when I was ten years old."

"Oh, really? How much is in it now?"

"Twenty-five dollars. I withdrew the interest."

We cracked up laughing.

"You're very thrifty," I complimented him.

"Look at it this way. If I saved everything, I couldn't afford to take your picture and buy you a yogurt."

We took the stairs up to the yogurt shop because Ted said the escalator was too slow and we didn't have enough time to glide around. However, we walked up the stairs so slowly and stopped so often to giggle that the escalator would probably have been ten times as fast. Once when Ted touched me he said, "You must be freezing. Look at those goosebumps. Don't you ever wear anything practical?" He ran his hand down my bare arm and my thoughts were anything but practical. "Not a dress to eat frozen yogurt in," said Ted firmly. He peeled off his scruffy jacket and draped it over my shoulders. The lining was warm from Ted's body. I shivered inside it though, and when I began eating the frozen yogurt — which was unexpectedly yummy — I shivered even more.

"Maybe you have malaria," suggested Ted.

We laughed even more. We walked to the rail of the second floor concourse and looked down on the egg stage. The camellias were dots of dark red and deep pink, and the organ was just a wooden box with wires.

"Do you write your articles using your own name?" I asked him.

"Yep. Townsend H. Mollison."

"I thought that might be you. I saw the by-line on the article about the citizen's protest on environmental budget cuts." Townsend H. Mollison, I thought. It was a name that cried out for an important door and brass letters on it.

"It's kind of a heavy name for high school," said Ted, "but it'll look great someday when I win a Pulitzer Prize."

We didn't laugh at that one. Should I tell him about the dream I had? I thought. About going to Nashville and cutting a record?

But down below me the organ salesman was signaling furiously. There was no time in my schedule to share anything. There was only time to thank Ted and run down the stairs. I felt like Cinderella leaving the ball. The prince stayed and she had to go back to her cruel stepmother's and work and slave.

At least I knew I would have an appreciative audience for this part of my concert. I slid onto the bench and put on violins and flutes instead of marching band trumpets. I began filling the mall with my engagement party repertoire.

I played for so many engagement parties and weddings that I have them on the brain. I guess any girl daydreams about them, but I have more to go on. Sometimes, when I'm in a bad mood, I daydream that my boyfriend and I skip all that junk and just get married. Sometimes, though, I plan this extravaganza with all the lace and flowers and hearts imaginable.

It was difficult to imagine Ted in a lace and flowers setting.

He was definitely the type to go to a judge some afternoon and wrap the whole thing up in five minutes.

Quit daydreaming about a wedding, you dodo, I told myself. The boy so far has bought you one frozen yogurt.

I wondered what Ted was daydreaming about. He must still be up on the balcony, eating his yogurt in peace. Perhaps he was having a second one, since he liked them so much. I decided next time Daddy and I went shopping I would stock up on frozen yogurts. Just in case.

After all, if nobody at Ted's house ever bought any food, he might come to mine to eat.

I played "Some Enchanted Evening" and hoped that Ted was duly enchanted. I could not twist around to look up and see.

". . . arrange monthly payments if you like," said the organ salesman to a plump elderly lady who was loving every note I played. I wished I could read the expression on Ted's face as easily.

". . . makes it look easy," said the old lady doubtfully, "but I'm not so sure it really is."

I thought that the next time Ted and I got together I would point out to him that we wore the exact same kind of watch: a big fat Timex with a sweep hand and numbers you could read from a yard away. All the girls I know have these itty-bitty watches that don't tell time; they just decorate the wrist. Then I started thinking about wrists, and how mine looked so slender and fair against Ted's, which was almost twice as large.

Within half an hour the camellia crowd had vanished. There was just a girl in gaudy red, an organ, and a thousand camellias on a stage. The organ man decided it was time to call it a day.

I ended my last love song with a flourish and looked up for Ted.

"Thanks a bunch," said the organ man. "You were terrific, honey. Give me your phone number. I'll want to have you regular, okay?"

All over the mall stores were closing down after the short Sunday hours. Huge metal gates clanked and great glass doors slid closed. The mall emptied.

There was no Townsend H. Mollison anywhere.

Beside me on the bench, yogurt was melting in a paper cup.

The only man who'd stayed around was, as usual, somebody who wanted me for my music.

12.

The next month was like a seesaw. I didn't go anywhere, but I had motion sickness.

I could not believe how many times my mind ran over my few conversations with Ted Mollison. Kept pretending I had not knocked him over or crashed heads with him or had trouble chewing in front of him. Kept working and reworking the talk we had had over the frozen yogurt, saying all these brilliant meaningful things that let him realize I was the girl for him.

But the phone didn't ring. Unless it was Ralph.

Ralph developed the habit of kissing me after a gig. "Love ya," he'd say, and then he'd drive me home. I wanted to screech at him: You do not love me, you love my music!

We did a gig where this really darling couple wanted their song played. None of us, not even Ralph, knew the song. "You know it, Alison," said the couple. "It's the one that goes *dum dum, daah, diddle diddle dum dum*"

I was doomed to spend the rest of my life listening to people sing *dum dum daaah diddle did-*

dle dum dum at me. Doomed to be kissed only by a fellow musician who figured it was cheaper than paying me more money for a good performance.

On top of everything else we lost our drummer, Alec. He was taking uppers to stay awake and downers to go to sleep; his performance had gotten so bad and his attendance was so unreliable that Ralph had to can him. It depressed me terribly.

And I felt so old, helping to break in another drummer.

I wandered around the halls at school, feeling so completely out of it. Sometimes I wondered if I had a cane and arthritis and looked eighty-three, and that was why none of these sixteen- and seventeen-year-olds hung out with me.

"What's the matter, Alison?" said Mike Mac-Bride one day. He was with a sophomore named Kimmy. "You look kind of down these days," said Mike with concern.

I liked Mike. I liked his concern for me. But I felt detached.

"Lost your dazzle, huh, Alison?" said Kimmy, who did not like Mike's worrying about me.

"I guess I don't have enough energy to dazzle all the time," I told them.

"So long as you can sparkle at night," said Kimmy, "when it counts." She smiled and led Mike away as if he were the tiny one and she the football player. It looked like a very nice skill to have. Wouldn't pay as well as music, of course, but clearly it was a lot more fun.

The beginning of spring had mating significance in my high school. Everybody I knew now came in pairs. Boys who had never before even wanted to walk down the same hall as a bunch of dumb old girls were now dating regularly and happily. Girls who had been nice and pretty and unnoticed were now nice and pretty and going steady.

Mike was not exactly going steady with Kimmy. I'd made it a point to keep up with things better since not even knowing about Kathleen's move. Mike was playing the field: a different girl every weekend. He always smiled at me and waved. And I always smiled back and waved from my end of the hall, too.

And then I'd wonder why Ted never called me.

Got a girlfriend, I thought. After all, it isn't treason to your girlfriend to go comfort some dumb girl who's weeping all over a shopping mall. He probably told his girlfriend about buying me a yogurt and giving me a Kleenex, and they probably had a good laugh about the bruise on his forehead where we batted skulls.

Dick Fraccola and Frannie were practically glued together now. She never asked me anymore about what my parties were like. I didn't know if she had enough parties of her own now, or if I had bored her too often and she didn't care what I did.

Sometimes I'd go for a whole day without thinking about Ted. Then I'd see the afternoon paper and begin wondering if he had an article in it, and I'd scour every page looking. And when I found one I'd read it at least twice. Ted was obviously sent to cover the dreary stuff nobody else wanted. I began finding out all about school board meetings and dog vaccination clinics.

Ridiculous, ridiculous, I'd scold myself. Ted isn't the only man in the world. Look around. Fall for somebody you're at least going to see more than twice a year.

There were even times when I felt this deep anger at Ted, as if he had done something to me by not calling me back. No matter that I reminded myself Ted hadn't even hinted that he wanted to date me. I still got angry with him for not calling.

It occurred to me that I could call him.

After all, I still had his number. Had it memorized, in fact.

And I had plenty of reasons to call. There was the article, for example. It hadn't come out yet. I could call to ask about it. I could tell him I owed him a Kleenex and a yogurt. I rehearsed it. "Hey, Ted, since neither of us has any free time, how about scheduling some official time together? Say, Saturday night at the movies?"

I considered myself about as liberated as any girl at J.F.K. High School. I earned a living. I mixed with some fairly rough crowds to do it. I handled school and a career. I got to and from places on my own, without help. I had my future planned.

And I couldn't — I *couldn't* — pick up a silly telephone to chat with a boy I liked.

Every night I'd stare at that rotten phone and move closer to it (as if it were a trap) and think: eight-six-nine, six-one-seven-eight. And every night I did not dial.

In each academic class we got our preliminary final grades. Don't you love Guidance Department jargon? "Preliminary final." Good grief.

Anyway, I had all A's except a B-plus in Latin. I stared at my little cards and wondered why I was doing any of this. Thursday night we had a dinner dance for the Elks' Club. Friday night, a wedding. Saturday, school dance.

We got new costumes which I detested: midnight blue satin pants and vest over a white satin blouse. The sleeves of the blouse were tight with squares of lace set in. There was something about the see-through quality of the sleeves that made them sexy, although it's difficult to think of one's arms as being sexy. Maybe it was just the whole idea of something half-hidden, half-revealed.

I fixed my hair in its most complex style, which took me half of Saturday afternoon, but after all I had nothing else to do. For once I didn't have any homework hanging over my head. I stared at myself in the mirror while I waited for Ralph to come pick me up.

"You're beautiful," said Daddy. He always says that, in just the same tone of voice. It has about as much meaning as Ralph's kisses. "How come you're not happy?" he said softly.

It bothered me terribly that he could tell. I had thought I was pretty good at hiding it. "It shows?" I said lightly. "I'd better cheer up before Ralph gets here. He doesn't like sad sacks on stage with him. Upsets the customers."

"Open up, honey," said my father. "What's wrong, anyway?"

Do you know I didn't try to figure how to explain what was wrong? I began planning sentences that would *hide* what was wrong.

How am I going to solve anything that way? I thought, and my eyes blurred over with tears. "I don't know, Daddy. I guess I'm just lonely."

Daddy sat down on the bed next to me and hugged me fiercely.

We didn't say anything after that.

But just pressing up against each other was comforting. Daddy knew and he understood, and I felt better for confessing. It didn't change anything. It just made the loneliness easier.

"This Ted ever call you back?" he said softly.

"Ted?" I repeated, as if it were a foreign word.

"You telephoned him, what, ten times? And floated upstairs after you finally got together with him."

"I did not float."

"Alison, there's nothing wrong with liking a boy. In fact, I was getting nervous because you didn't seem to like any."

"Oh, Daddy, I like them all. But none of them like me back. Especially Ted. I don't even *know* Ted, I . . ." I broke off then. Confession was fine, but even to my father — maybe especially to my father — I couldn't say how I felt about Ted.

"You had that date with him," coaxed Daddy.

"It wasn't a date. It was just an interview."

"Oh," said my father. He didn't seem to be able to think of anything more to say. I knew the feeling.

And then Ralph was outside leaning on his horn.

"'Bye, pet," said my father. "Have fun anyway." He grinned at me hopefully.

"I will," I promised him. And the odd thing was, I knew I would. I could feel my depression lifting, feel my musical engine gearing up, getting ready to give these customers the best music they could possibly buy.

I slid into the van next to Ralph. He gave me a very peculiar look, as if I were not the person he had expected. Then he smiled slightly and turned his attention to his driving.

"What?" I demanded.

"What, what?"

"What did you look at me like that for?"

Ralph smiled again. It was not his usual evil grin, but a nice funny smile. I had never seen him with that expression. I wondered if he planned to fire me and get another, older, more seasoned musician.

"Someday, Alison," he said softly. "Someday."

"Someday, what?" I really was cross with Ralph. He'd punctured my revving up and obviously he was going to be mysterious and not tell me what his funny look had meant. Men.

"Someday," explained Ralph, turning left, "you're going to knock 'em dead, lady."

I made a face. "Someday!" I huffed at him. "Who wants someday? How about tonight? That's when I want to knock 'em dead. Right now."

He grinned at me, evilly this time. I felt much more at ease with the old, mean Ralph and snarled back at him. "You have a chance," he told me. "We're going to play for your peers tonight."

"Honestly, Ralph, getting answers out of you is like pulling my feet out of day-old cement. What are you talking about?"

"Western High is having a dance tonight. Remember? That's why we boned up on heavy rock last week."

I remembered. I had thought Rob's junior high

band room would collapse under the vibrations. "Did you say Western High?" I asked Ralph.

"Yup."

Ted's school.

Nobody goes to a dance without a date. If Ted were there, he'd be there with his girlfriend.

I didn't have enough problems. Tonight I'd have to watch the one boy I'd ever really been fascinated by dance with somebody else. And I'd have to supply the music to be danced by.

13.

There was some good news and some bad news about the dance at Western High.

The good news was that Ted was there without a date. When I saw him I thought my heart would flip out of my chest. All I could think of was: How am I going to keep Ralph's beat when my heart is beating away so loudly at a different rhythm?

He was better-looking than I had remembered. I had remembered him as tall and strong and warm and comforting. On top of that he was just plain attractive. His face crinkled into a grin when he saw me and he blew me a kiss.

I was playing at the time. I couldn't lift my fingers from the keyboard to blow one back, and I couldn't purse up and kiss the air because Ralph was watching me very suspiciously. I didn't want Ralph to know what I was feeling about Ted. Ralph is very big on teasing me. I could just imagine how he'd rejoice at the whole new world opening up: He'd be teasing me night and day about dear old Ted.

So I just grinned back at Ted.

That was the good news.

The bad news was that he had a camera, which he treated as lovingly as any mere girl could ever hope to be treated. Between shots Ted actually caressed it. "Yearbook photographer," he explained to me, grinning. He hopped around, getting good shots of dancers swirling past the bandstand. It was not difficult to imagine Ted dancing with his camera in preference to me.

You would think a boy alone at a dance would be lonely, but it was depressingly clear that Ted found a camera perfect company. I am very fond of the piano keyboard, but I don't *hug* it. I felt like being a Muppet. I'd make the scrunched-up sort of face Kermit the Frog makes when everything turns out wrong.

Behind the bandstand an enormous backdrop was painted in gaudy rainbow patches — fluorescent, sprinkled with glitter, glistening with bits of mirror. Our faces and clothing changed colors with the lights. Ralph was letting it all hang out and Rob hunched over his drums as if he were beating out his autobiography, and it was pretty seamy reading. Scores of couples rotated past us, completely caught up in the music.

Everybody but me, as a matter of fact, was caught up in the mood, energized by the rock beat. I was trying to watch old Ted.

"Ted," observed Lizzie, "is taking an awful lot of photographs of our keyboard player, Ralph. And she doesn't even go to this high school. What kind of yearbook pictures are these, anyway?"

I ignored Lizzie's teasing. Was Ted really taking photographs of me? I couldn't tell. There were

101

so many lights going on and off, so many splashes of color and noise, that I couldn't pick Ted's out.

He isn't taking any of me, I told myself. That would be dumb. He's got so many of me already his article can't possibly use more. Lizzie is just trying to get a rise out of me.

"How many times," said Ralph between phrases of melody, "do I have to tell you to keep your social life separated from your professional life?"

"Twice," I said with dignity. "That's the total number of times you have said that and each time I have paid close attention. Consider the subject closed."

Ralph and Lizzie snickered like seventh-graders. I got even with them by modulating between verses, which startled them completely and made it much harder for them to get through the piece. I knew it was war when Ralph picked the next number, a piece I'd specifically said in rehearsal I couldn't play well enough to do at the dance. I glared at Ralph and I was just getting into the glare — just really getting myself organized for a good, long glare — when Ted slipped through a gap in the canvas and sat on the floor next to my piano bench.

"Hi!" he yelled over our racket.

My glare slid around and fell off. "Oh," I said. "Hi, Ted."

He had to come up during a piece I couldn't play even in the best of circumstances. I felt Lizzie and Ralph watching me. If I lost the beat by talking with Ted I would never hear the end of it.

There wasn't even time to tell Ted we'd talk after this number. Ralph had us in it, throbbing and moving, and I had to blot Ted out of my mind.

At least, that was my theory. But when you have a mind like mine and a boy like Ted, it isn't so easy. Somehow the rock beat disintegrated into eight-six-nine, six-one-seven-eight.

When the piece was finally over and we broke for fifteen seconds to let the couples applaud, I looked at Ted. He was staring either at an overused extension cord plug or at my ankle. I told myself it was my sexy ankle that was attracting him, but instantly, as if Ralph had told him to do it, Ted unplugged one of the cords and took it off somewhere behind the painted screen to plug into a different — presumably safer — outlet.

I looked back down at my ankles. They *were* beautiful, if I do say so myself. (No one else ever has, I must admit.)

We launched into a slow number and kids began dancing in that slouching, rotating way that isn't dancing at all, just vertical hugging. The lucky girls were with taller guys and could sort of lean on their chests and let themselves be circled by long, strong arms for the dance. Ted, I thought, is taller than I am. We could dance like that.

My fingers played along by memory. I didn't seem to be guiding them at all. I couldn't decide if I had really hit my professional stride or if I was about to make a horrible series of mistakes by not paying enough attention.

Ted came back. I guessed I'd be making mistakes by not paying enough attention.

"No more pictures to take?" I said during a two-beat rest.

"Nope."

Ted began tapping out the rhythm on my left ankle.

I thought, if I even *live* through this piece, let alone play it right, that's all I ask.

Ralph was giving me some very fishy stares. I stared fishily right back. I really needed my foot back for the soft pedal but I decided in a dance room as big as this a soft pedal would be silly. Better by far to let Ted tickle my ankle.

"Who are you with?" I said, hoping to be absolutely sure about Ted's social commitments. "Doesn't she want to dance?"

"Not with anybody," said Ted. "I always mean to invite someone, but I never get around to it. Probably by the time I picked up the phone, the girl would be so insulted by being called so late she'd turn me down anyway."

Ted began a long involved story about how his newspaper work kept him so busy he couldn't manage a social life as well. I could have told him not to bother with the details; I knew them all, but I liked the sound of his voice.

I began fantasizing about dancing with Ted, since he was alone. Of course, it was a ridiculous fantasy, because without me there wouldn't be any music to dance *to*. Still, I had us both out there on the floor, in each other's arms, doing a slow number, and Ted's fingers tapping out a rhythm on a more interesting place than an ankle. Ted and I would make this beautiful wonderful couple, and we'd be so nice together that other couples would stop dancing and watch us, the way they do in movies. (I've certainly never seen anybody do that in real life.)

Then I had this horrible thought.

I no longer knew how to dance.

Oh, God, I prayed quickly. If Ted asks me to dance, teach me how in a hurry!

But he would not ask me, I really knew that. He knew I was working. He'd be disgusted if I asked him to go dancing when he was on his way to cover an important fire or something, so it would not occur to him to ask me when I was playing with the combo.

Though personally, I was quite sure that a dance with Ted would be infinitely preferable either to a fire or a music program.

Ralph leaned over the keyboard. "Get out of here, Ted old man. We're working."

My stomach turned into knots. Ralph was at his meanest and oldest. He was going to treat Ted like an obnoxious little boy and Ted would hold me responsible. He'd never come near me again all evening.

"Hi, Ralph," said Ted. "I'm the one who went and got your electric keyboard at that wedding, remember?"

Ralph grunted and gestured for Ted to leave. Gestured rudely.

Ted merely smiled. "I'm not bothering her, Ralph. Just sitting here."

Ralph gave Ted his meanest, most vicious smile and Ted gave Ralph his sweetest, most friendly smile. After another minute Ralph sighed and shrugged and went off to play his sax solo.

"Ted," I said, "I am truly impressed. Grown men quail before Ralph. Junior League presidents become incoherent. Politicians tremble. But you just sit there and smile."

"Some of us have it," said Ted expansively, "and some of us don't."

I didn't think I'd get through the next piece for laughing. I was so tickled with Ted. Imagine being able to stand up to Ralph! Ted sort of sprawled on the second and third levels of the bandstand as if he were at the beach, sunning himself, and watched me play. I was very self-conscious and yet I was enjoying every second of it. I was very, very sure Ted wasn't interested in the music I was providing. He was interested in me.

In our next little break between numbers, Lizzie said, "At least the kid is making Alison smile, Ralph. She's worth any two klieg lights up here, beaming away at Ted."

"Yecch," said Ralph.

I blushed painfully. Was it that obvious that I was so delighted to have Ted up there? I looked over at Ted again. He winked at me and said to Ralph, "Can you do a number without keyboard, Ralph? Alison and I want to dance."

Ralph almost choked. He actually sputtered into his mouthpiece and had to grab at Lizzie's bass for support.

"I think he means no," said Lizzie helpfully.

My ankles began jiggling of their own accord, nervous and excited. Ted had actually asked me to dance! Or at least, he had asked Ralph for permission to let me dance with him. How old-fashioned, I thought. As if Ralph is my father and Ted has to ask for my hand.

During our next number I tried to watch the dance floor as well as watch Ted and pay attention to the notes. I needed to get clues on dancing.

Unfortunately every girl seemed to have her own style. I was much too clunky on my feet to develop instant style.

What if we actually dance, I thought, and I trip on Ted's feet and we fall again? I've made him fall once and I've given him a bashed head once.

I really would have to quit the combo if that happened. Lizzie and Ralph would tease me unmercifully, and besides, I would be locked up in my bedroom not forgiving myself for being so stupid and uncoordinated.

Since speech was impossible during a rock number, Ted passed me a note, holding it so I could read it. Instead of *May I have the next dance?* Ted had scribbled, *May I have the next band break?*

I nodded.

He likes me, I thought. In spite of everything he really likes me. All the girls here and it's my company he wants.

Of course, all the other girls here had dates. I was actually the only girl his age who was unattached, so if I wanted to be cynical about it, what choice did Ted have except me?

Ted went back to work on my ankles, but he got tired of them quickly and began edging up. Ralph and his sax moseyed over to my side of the piano this time and Ralph stepped on Ted's hand. Not very gently, either. Ralph and I kept playing. Ted laughed. I said, "Ralph, cut it out."

"Ted," said Ralph warningly.

"I know, I know. Leave, or you'll assign me to detention class." Ted vanished behind the painted screen.

It was just as well. Ralph was so mad I think he would have broken Ted's fingers in a minute. "Alison," he said, "do you have any idea how much these kids had to raise to pay us?"

"I know exactly how much they paid," I said. "They're paying part of it to me, remember."

"*I* remember perfectly," said Ralph sharply. "Do *you*?"

He was really and truly angry with me. My daydreams about Ted faded. I was here as part of a combo, that was true, and I had no right to play personal games and risk ruining a professional engagement. "I'm sorry, Ralph," I mumbled. My cheeks hurt with a blush so fierce I felt burned.

"I know you like him," said Ralph quietly. "But not on my time."

Ralph had never been so fatherly. I hated it. My own father would not have bawled me out like that. I felt so *public*. Five hundred dancing kids were watching us. Of course, they couldn't hear, didn't know what Ralph was saying — probably thought he was announcing the next number to me — but I felt spied on. Exposed.

I struggled through the next piece. It was only three minutes long, I guess, but it felt like an hour. My fingers felt heavy, like metal slugs breaking the ivory. And I was going to cry again, I knew it like the voice of doom. In public, on a stage!

I gritted my teeth and concentrated on the notes and the beat.

"All right, all right," said Ralph. "You win. Go find your pal Ted and dance the next number. I'll do the piano."

"You know how to play piano?" I said, amazed.

"Alison, would I own one if I couldn't use it?" He sat down literally before I could get up, nudging me right off the bench — into Ted.

If we'd rehearsed that we couldn't have done it better! Ted caught me, pulling me down off the bottom level of the bandstand and onto the dance floor. He was grinning from ear to ear. "Old Ralph's bark is worse than his bite, huh?" he said. The floor was very crowded up near the band so Ted locked his fingers around my wrist and hauled me off to a more secluded spot. I cooperated. I certainly didn't want to dance for the first time in two years right in front of my combo!

"Hey, Ted," said a boy near our spot, "you're supposed to lead, not shove."

He and his girlfriend burst out laughing at us.

I bit my lips, but Ted only laughed back. "You can't lead in a dance like this. All you can do is demonstrate." He demonstrated, twitching, wiggling, and thrusting wildly.

"Well," said the girl, still laughing, "you're supposed to stop short of bodily mutilation."

The girl was shorter than I was and had the friendliest smile! I liked her right away. I stopped blushing and started laughing, too. Ted and I were pretty funny, with him dancing so insanely and me afraid to try. "I'm Cindy," she said to me, "and this is Jon."

We beamed at each other. "I'm Alison. I'm with the band."

"I know," said Cindy. "We noticed you. You're not wearing the sort of clothes anybody could overlook. Ted," she asked him, "how you've changed. The last I knew, the only girl you cared about was the one who could do your enlargements cheap."

Next thing *I* knew, the four of us were standing over by the refreshments talking as if we were old friends, and Ted had gotten me a ginger ale and Cindy shared her cup of M & M candies with me. I stared back at the band for a minute. I did not feel as if I knew anybody up there. In their vivid, gaudy costumes, making their wild noisy music, they looked like a race apart. I'm not the music tonight, I thought. My wish came true. I'm the guest, I'm the date.

Jon said, "It's remarkable, isn't it, Cindy? Ted Mollison. Actually participating in normal high school life. He's even dancing. With a real, live, attractive girl."

Cindy snorted. "I wouldn't call it dancing," she said, and we all laughed. I felt like a soda bottle that had been shaken up: Open me and I'd fizz all over the place.

When the number ended it was like Cinderella in reverse. Cinderella had to go back to an ordinary life, but I had to hurry back to the palace.

We played another hour, I guess. It didn't feel like me playing. *I* was out there with Ted, holding his hand, meeting his friends, laughing at his jokes.

Ted was clearly a person with a lot of extra energy and no hang-ups whatsoever about doing things in public. He actually climbed to the top of the closed-up bleachers way at the rear of the gymnasium and began making semaphorelike signals at me. None of his classmates so much as blinked an eye. It must have been normal behavior. "Good grief," said Lizzie, as Ted turned his entire body into an alphabet spelling out A-L-I-S-O-N (the N nearly killed him). "Can't you do better than that, Alison?" she wanted to know.

I looked at Ted, who was vaulting down at last, being applauded by some of his friends, bowing to them.

"No," I said. "No, I don't think I can do better than that!"

14.

"Are you putting me on?" said Frannie. "You have a date for *breakfast*?"

Like a dope I had told one girl — a reasonably pleasant, seemingly trustworthy person who shared a gym locker with me on Thursdays — that I was going to have breakfast with Ted. She had told everybody she had ever met, heard of or seen in her entire life.

"Alison," said Jan, shaking her head either in admiration or disgust. "I couldn't even get my hair brushed by six-thirty. Are you seriously going to be up, dressed, fixed, and able to speak in words of more than one syllable by six-thirty in the morning?"

"With a reporter," pointed out Frannie, "she'll even have to be articulate."

That was in the hall. In my next class Phyllis said, "You should at least have made this date for Saturday morning instead of during the school week. Then you could have your breakfast at a more respectable hour. Six-thirty in the morning! Really, Alison!"

And after that class Mike's girlfriend, Kimmy, said, "Romance does not occur at breakfast." I listened to her mostly because I figured Kimmy knew a lot more about romance than I did. All I knew were the lyrics of a thousand songs. Kimmy knew firsthand. "At brunch, you could have romance, yes. At luncheons, dinners, cocktails, and after-theater drinks. But not at breakfast."

"Why," said Lisa, "didn't you make this date for Saturday morning?"

"Because he's leaving Friday afternoon for a seminar on Creative Journalism in the Small City."

Everybody was momentarily diverted by having to protest that we did not live in a small city. This led to definitions of what a city might be and everybody had to shut up when Janey, who is from Manhattan, told us what a city was. Not our town, she said firmly.

And then in Latin, Ms. Gardener actually said that she promised not to call on me the day of my breakfast date. "Since you'll be too busy during breakfast to do your translation," she explained.

"How did you know I do my translations during breakfast?" I said.

"Just a lucky guess."

The class howled with laughter.

And the strangest thing was, they were laughing at me — and yet it didn't bother me at all. I rather enjoyed it. Ted's whole high school had laughed at his antics during the dance, and Ted just figured the laughs were their way of saying they liked him. Ted, just by asking me out, had given me confidence that performing music never had. I felt ten times stronger than I had a week ago.

We hadn't meant to date over breakfast, of course.

We'd compared engagement calendars and the only free evening for both of us was actually eleven days off. Ted frowned at my calendar and said firmly that *he* wasn't going to wait any eleven days!

Technically speaking, Ralph drove me home from that dance in his van, but actually, I floated home. On Ted's words.

And no amount of teasing in school could puncture my balloon.

"I guess I wasn't creative enough," said Mike MacBride. "It just didn't occur to me to ask you out for scrambled eggs at dawn." He was smiling at me, with the funny gentle smile he had.

I didn't know what to make of his remark. He had never asked me anywhere for anything, just hinted vaguely that he might. I wondered if he was just teasing, in his nice easygoing way, or if he really meant that he wished he had asked me out.

All my thoughts about Ted quivered. I was crazy about Ted . . . and yet, I'd been crazy about Mike my entire life. What if Mike wanted to ask me out?

What would I really do if my dreams came true and *two* wonderful boys wanted my company?

But Mike was going off with Kimmy, so that one was likely to remain a daydream.

Ted and I were going to have this breakfast date at my house, a factor I omitted to tell anybody at school. I don't drive, and if Ted came to pick me up and we drove somewhere, there wouldn't be time to eat before we'd both have to go on to our separate schools.

My father was so delighted at the idea his little girl was going to have a date (and under his supervision) that he didn't even comment on the odd hour. He just said that along with the usual frozen doughnuts we thaw each morning in the microwave, he — my very own good father — would demonstrate his affection by laying in frozen bagels, frozen waffles, bacon strips, and instant maple-sugar–flavored oatmeal.

I asked Daddy if he planned to be present.

He looked very hurt and said if he didn't have breakfast he would collapse at work, and besides, I made terrible coffee and he had to get up to make it himself.

I said the coffee was instant and nobody could make it any more terrible than when it came out of the jar.

He said, well, he would come down in a new bathrobe, how was that? And I said, that was perfect.

The night before this breakfast date Ralph called up. I could tell by his voice that he was up to no good so I was suspicious of everything he said, which was a good thing, because he tried to con me into a gig. "Did I remember to tell you I promised the Men's Breakfast Prayer Meeting that you'd play hymns for them tomorrow? They're not paying anything, of course, but I told them you were free and you'd love to do it."

115

"Very funny, Ralph."

About half an hour later Lizzie called. "I just spoke to Ted," she said ominously.

She'd do that, too. Lizzie would stop at nothing. "Did he survive?" I said weakly.

"I told him his schedule was altogether too crowded and he would just have to omit something."

"What did you suggest he should omit?" I asked, although I had a pretty good idea.

"You," said Lizzie, and she laughed until I had to hang up on her.

"And they pretend to be adults," said my father. "Those musicians of yours are infantile and immature."

I agreed with that. I sat trying to do homework so I wouldn't be worried all through my Ted breakfast about not having done my math. Instead of doing the math, though, I worried about what I would say to Ted. Would having Daddy there make it difficult? What if we couldn't think of anything to say to each other? What if the whole thing consisted of me saying, "How about some more orange juice, Ted?" and Ted saying, "No, thanks, Alison, prune juice is fine."

I decided Kimmy was right. You couldn't bring up romantic subjects at breakfast. Breakfast was not romantic. At breakfast, I thought, Ted will see the real me for the first time. Not me performing and not me rehearsing. Me eating frozen waffles.

The phone rang again and I knew it would be Rob this time, probably coached by Ralph and Lizzie about what to tease old Alison about this time.

116

But it was Frannie, who wanted to know what I was planning to wear.

"Wear?" I said, as if I usually went around naked.

"On your breakfast date," she said impatiently. "What sort of costume?"

"Oh, for heaven's sake. We're both going on to school afterward. I'm just wearing school clothes, I guess. Oxford shirt, skirt, Shetland sweater."

Frannie was disappointed. She had actually thought I would have a costume, as if this were a gig, and I had to be spangled and special. "My personality," I told her, "is all the flash I need."

Frannie laughed. "Alison, you are too much."

She was too much. Frankly, this breakfast thing was more pressure than I had bargained for. All the confidence Ted had given me by asking me out was dwindling away because of everybody's interest.

"You know Todd Morrell and Bobby Bastien?" said Frannie.

"Yes."

"You've started a trend. They're taking Shelley and Margo to breakfast Friday."

Me, Alison, setting a trend with her first date.

I decided definitely not to tell anybody that my father in his new bathrobe was present for the entire thing.

"Actually," said Ted, "I already ate breakfast."

My father stared at Ted and then at the mounds of food he'd bought for Ted to gobble up. Ted said nervously, "My mother has this rule. I don't leave in the morning without hot food in my stomach."

We just stared at him. A breakfast date and he'd already eaten? Oh no, I thought, it's going to be a nightmare, not a dream. I looked at the clock. The forty-five minutes we had began to look like very long minutes.

"My mother is very suspicious of other people's nutritional standards," he said. He was flushed. Embarrassment? I thought. "I have to brown-bag it to school instead of buying hot lunch because she knows I'll be filling my system with preservatives, saccharin, and artificial food coloring."

My father said, "I would have to agree with her there. Alison and I like to think we're sort of guinea pigs for cancer-causing agents, we eat so many of them."

Ted and my father got along just fine. In fact, they sat there for fifteen solid minutes, one-third of my breakfast date, exchanging quips. I thought, This is the pits. It's one thing to be envious of Kimmy and Frannie and all the rest. Now I have to be jealous of my own father?

But I couldn't seem to think of anything interesting to say. My father was filled with funny remarks and Ted kept topping them, and the two of them had a fine old time. I poured myself a cup of coffee and drank it black, which I absolutely hate, for punishment. Coffee makes me feel hot from the inside out, the opposite of sunshine, which makes me hot from the outside in. That was the sort of thing I thought about, while Ted and my father had a date.

"Well," said my father suddenly, pushing away from the table, "guess I'd better get ready for work." And he was gone, thundering up the stairs, so nobody could mistake the fact that Ted and I were now alone.

The good conversation stopped.

Ted and I just sort of looked at each other and smiled edgily.

"You look terrific," said Ted.

"Thank you."

"In fact, I was sitting here thinking a camera crew would be arriving soon to film you for a floor wax ad."

"A what?" I said.

"You know. Where the unbelievably well-dressed superwoman, wife, and mother, who has a full-time glamorous career, waxes her floor just before the prime minister comes to dinner and she doesn't even get her satin slippers spotted?"

I giggled. "I'm not that familiar with floor wax."

Ted made a big production of examining our kitchen floor. "No. I don't think you are."

"I have better things to do than wax floors, Ted Mollison."

And that led us into a discussion of things we'd rather do than housework, which Mrs. Mollison felt her sons should do instead of her. I was all for Mrs. Mollison's getting out of housework, but I did feel sorry for Ted having to do any. Housework is such drudgery.

"Sorry enough for me that we could have a housecleaning date?" said Ted hopefully. "Me wash windows, you polish silver?"

"Not that sorry."

We laughed. Ted took a piece of Sara Lee coffeecake after all, and we munched happily, poured more coffee, and talked about dusting (the evils of it).

Right in the middle of his next sentence Ted leaped up. "Committee meeting!" he said. "Forgot the time. Alison, I have to run. I'll call you." He was already elbowing into his jacket, gathering up his books and his ever-present camera. "Thanks," he said at the door, and for 'a moment we stared at each other.

Kiss me, I thought.

But he didn't. He shifted his books to his other side and said again, looking at the dusty venetian blinds at the window, "Thanks, Alison." And then he was gone.

I watched him drive away.

I was so exhausted by the whole thing I was ready for bed again. It was only seven forty-five and I had an entire day of school ahead. A day in which an awful lot of people would be wanting to know what a breakfast date was like. I tried to think of a good catchy answer I would toss at everybody. "Well," I'd say casually, "we sloshed a lot of coffee around, that's all."

I wondered if that *was* all. Or if Ted would call again for a longer, better date than one slice of Sara Lee and a few minutes chatter about dust.

Ted's car turned the far corner of our street and he honked twice. Good-bye, I thought; that wasn't a honk at another car, that was a honk good-bye to me.

All day long in school I could hear the horn beeping at me.

15.

Ted did not call me.

On Saturday night he just appeared. We were supplying background dinner music at a fund drive kickoff for a new Y.M.C.A. We'd had three speeches — boring — and now they were asking for pledges — boring. Most of the people there were not physical fitness types. They were stodgy, moneyed types. I was yawning to myself over the keyboard. We had to play very softly and Rob was just sort of diddling at the drums and we were all in danger of falling asleep over our own music — and there in the doorway was Ted.

The first thing I noticed was that he did not have a camera with him. He looked almost undressed without it dangling from a cord around his neck. I envied his poise, the way he simply smiled at the dinner organizers and threaded his way through the pledge-takers, around the tables, and over to me.

He gave Ralph a quick look, obviously worrying that Ralph might throw him out. "Not to worry," I whispered. "Ralph is so bored he wouldn't mind if you hung from the chandeliers."

Immediately Ted looked up at the ceiling for good chandeliers to hang from, but all there were were long white strips of fluorescent lights. Ted looked disappointed.

Ted found a folding chair and sat next to me. I moved a little on my piano bench but he didn't take me up on it. "I promised your father not to bother you on the job," he whispered. "I think that includes taking a separate seat."

So he had called Daddy to see where I was tonight!

It made me all warm and excited to think about that call. About Ted wanting to be around me, talking to my father, getting in his car, and driving out here just to come sit with me.

Get closer, Ted, I thought. I love you for your long, lean legs.

But Ted stayed where he was, on the gray metal folding chair.

"What's in your hair?" said Ted.

"Stars."

"That's what I thought they were. Why do you have stars in your hair? How do they stick?"

"Decorated hair is in this year. Ribbons, combs, bangles, beads, and even stars. They come in a jar — you just shake them on right after you spray on the hairspray and they stick."

We played the theme from *Ordinary People*. The best scene in that film was where the boy, Con, lies in bed rehearsing the phone call he'll make to the girl he wants to date. I wondered if it had been hard for Ted to call my father. Somehow, I couldn't picture Ted having trouble phoning people or walking into rooms filled with strange people.

"I'm not sure I like them," said Ted.

I thought he meant rooms full of strange people.

"The stars in your hair," he explained. "They don't look very strokable."

That time I really did miss a beat in the music. It was a perfectly simple phrase that I'd played perhaps a thousand times, and I fumbled it. Ted noticed it; Ralph noticed it; in fact, I think the whole room noticed it. I stared down into the keys and waited for the repeat to come so I could set it right.

I'd set my hair with my electric curlers and I was wearing it loose, which I don't usually do, because it falls forward into my face and makes it impossible to see what I'm doing. But there was enough hair spray in my hair to make each strand like wire.

And tonight Ted Mollison wanted to stroke it.

I wondered if Lizzie would lend — or even sell — me her hairbrush so I could brush it all out during a break.

Ted said softly, "You really look fantastic."

It was a good thing he said that during a rest. My hands began to dampen. I tried to think of what to suggest to do after the music. Ted obviously had his car. Ralph always took me home, but tonight I'd go home with Ted.

Ted didn't talk to me again, but I could feel him there, only inches away, looking at me and thinking about me. I had sat on a hundred stages in front of a lot of audiences but I had never felt the spotlight as much as I did then. I could hardly breathe. A good thing I wasn't a singer!

When we broke up Ted went to get my jacket, and Ralph said to me, "You want we should keep on playing so you two can have a little music to make love by?"

"Ralph!" I said furiously.

"Well, you're making it awfully obvious, dear," said Lizzie.

"How about Ted?" I asked her. "Is he making it obvious?"

"He came, didn't he?" said Lizzie.

I decided she was right. He had come; that made it obvious. He liked me, too. Ralph left by himself, after informing Ted at length that it sure was a pleasure not to have to tote Alison around anymore, and why didn't Ted show up every night like this and set Ralph free? Ted just grinned, but he didn't commit himself to every night.

We sat by the piano and talked until the dinner organizers asked us very politely did we have rides home? Because it was getting very late and they really did have to lock up.

I was amazed to see that Ted and I had talked for an entire *hour* after Ralph and the rest had left. I could not believe it. Ted was so easy and companionable I really had not noticed the time. "Come on," said Ted, "I'll drive you home."

"You . . . you want to stop off somewhere?" I said. It was also amazing how much courage it took me to ask him that. "We . . . we could get ice cream, or something." Ted hesitated, and I said, "My treat."

"Actually," he said, "I'm in a popcorn mood. Where can we go besides the movies where we can get popcorn?"

"My house."

So we went to my house. Ted, it turned out, was forbidden to have popcorn at home. His mother hated the smell. She thought popcorn smelled like Woolworth's, and that made her think of unwashed shoplifters getting their popcorn out of a machine using fake butter.

"I," I told Ted, "supply nothing but the most high-class popcorn with real butter."

We talked all the way home, too, and it was like a television script. I thought everything Ted said was funny and he thought everything I said was hysterical. We kept laughing and enjoying each other and I actually felt giddy, I was enjoying myself so much.

When we got to our driveway and pulled up behind the fat old fir trees between the house and the garden, Ted turned off the motor and the lights and we sat for a moment in silence and darkness.

I wanted to kiss Ted so much I could hardly stand it, but I wanted *him* to kiss *me*, so I just sat there. We looked at each other and I could feel him holding his breath, too, and I thought, Go ahead, do it. But he got out of the car and came around to open my door, and the moment was gone. Daddy heard us and turned on the porch lights and yelled for us to come on in. The three of us popped popcorn, and the three of us joked and talked together, and the three of us had a wonderful time.

125

The only trouble was, I would rather that just two of us had that wonderful time.

"I wonder if the space shuttle is doing okay," said Ted. I blinked at him, because nobody had expressed any interest in space shuttles up till then and the remark had nothing to do with anything.

My father said, "I don't know. It'll be on the news, though. You want me to turn it on? There's a set downstairs and another up."

I said, "Your TV upstairs is a better one, Daddy."

My father looked at me for a moment, and then at Ted, and then he laughed. "So it is," he said. "Enjoy your popcorn."

He went on upstairs, and Ted and I were alone in the unwaxed kitchen with the rest of the popcorn. "Are you really interested in the space shuttle?" I asked. "Or was that a ploy?"

"I'm interested in everything," said Ted, and he proceeded to tell me all the things he was interested in. I felt as if we could talk for a decade and not begin to say all the things we wanted to say to each other. I had forgotten, really, how wonderful it is to share things with a person your own age, who has your own ideas.

Ted handed me a napkin when the popcorn was finally gone — we'd popped a huge batch — and when our fingers touched I shivered. For one moment it was just like in the car, both of us holding our breath, and then Ted was leaning across the table and we were kissing each other. I loved touching him. We moved the chairs and got closer and kissed again. "Tastes of popcorn and butter and salt," said Ted, laughing softly.

126

"Want a glass of water?" I said, embarrassed.

"Definitely not. I'll just kiss away the rest of the popcorn till I get down to the real Alison."

We started to go into the living room, to sit on the couch and be more comfortable, but we never got there. We just stood between the stove and the refrigerator and hugged and kissed.

"I was right," said Ted after a bit. "You can't stroke stars."

We were both gasping for breath. It wasn't that kissing was so strenuous. It was just that I was so glad to have it happen I couldn't seem to fill my lungs. I put my hands on Ted's shoulders and I wanted to hang on to him all night.

My father yelled, "I've finished my popcorn. Have you?"

"No," yelled Ted, "not yet, sir."

My father shouted, "Well, I have, and I'm coming down to wash up the popcorn popper."

"He's very considerate," said Ted. "Now my mother, she would have inched up on us to see what we were up to."

We gave each other a short hard hug and moved back to our separate places at the table. It felt so funny to be sitting opposite each other instead of next to each other. I felt as if those kisses should have cemented us together so that we never sat opposite each other again.

We didn't kiss good-bye. My father was there.

Fathers certainly know how to kiss. And my father certainly knew we hadn't been chomping popcorn the whole time he was upstairs. But I could not bring myself to get close enough to Ted for a good-bye kiss. I did not know Ted well enough to announce how I felt about him by kiss-

127

ing in front of anybody. "Good night, Ted," said my father formally. "I hope we see you again."

And Ted said, "Yes, sir. Good night."

I lay on my bed for at least another hour before I fell asleep, thinking about boys and kisses and music and happiness.

Ted had not asked me for another date.

Did it mean he forgot? Or didn't want to commit himself? Or took those kisses much much more lightly than I did?

Or had my father's presence bothered him as much as it did me, so that he couldn't say anything except, "Yes, sir."

I got up and tossed the rest of the jar of stars into the wastebasket and promised myself that from now on my hair would always be soft and unsprayed and free of annoying stars.

I lay back down and thought about Ted some more and wondered if he was lying awake thinking about me. Or if he was planning a terrific feature with photographs for his newspaper and that was more interesting to him.

For the first time in my life, I really painfully wanted a mother. I even went downstairs and got the photograph of Mother in her wedding gown and I said to her, "I love somebody, Mother. It's scary."

My thoughts tumbled over each other, a lot of sorrow and joy mixed up together, and I finally went back up to bed, wondering if I would ever know Ted well enough to talk to him about my dead mother.

16.

The only male who telephoned me during the next week was Ralph. There may be a woman out there daydreaming of a phone call from Ralph, but it isn't me. When I heard his voice I just groaned.

He was just checking to be sure I knew that the hour of next Saturday's club date had been changed. Yes, I told him, I knew.

We had gigs Thursday, Friday, and Saturday. Ted didn't appear at any of them, he didn't call my father to ask where I was, and he didn't call me to arrange for us to be at the same place any night, either.

I felt flat all week, as if I had once been this plush stuffed toy and somebody ironed me, or punctured me. That evening had meant so much to me! How could it not have meant just as much to Ted?

I told myself I would just call Ted myself. This was the era of women's liberation. Just as soon as old Ralph stopped tying up my phone line I would call Ted. Why even bother to have a telephone if you're not going to call up the people you want to talk to, right?

Ralph said, "And please have Ted come and get you. I have a date and I don't want to have to drive you home."

There was no way I could telephone Ted and ask him if he could take up chauffeur work where Ralph was leaving off. I said, "Well, if he can't my father will, how's that?"

Ralph's life was now perfect.

My life dwindled into staring at the silent telephone, telling myself any fool could make a simple phone call. Hi, Ted, this is Alison. How about a movie?

Hi, Ted, how are you? I miss you, come spend an evening.

Hi, Ted, I have this unbelievable crush on you, don't stay away, come stay with me.

But Ted didn't call me and I didn't call him and it was my father who had to come and get me after the gig Saturday.

I hung on to my cloud of happiness by my fingernails, hoping Ted would reemerge without my having to dial him myself, but Monday had to intervene.

At first I thought it was just any old Monday, and I was usefully employing homeroom by doing the last line of my Latin translation. Everybody was buzzing around, and in spite of my dedication to Ovid's immortal lines, I could not avoid figuring out the topic of their conversation.

Yearbooks.

I wanted to die.

See, yearbooks have to be signed. Nobody wants a blank yearbook. You want a yearbook covered with the handwriting of all your intimate friends and admirers, so that none of the photographs are visible and all the pages testify to your immense popularity.

It works fine if you're immensely popular.

I said to myself, I'm a junior. I don't know that many seniors. It's okay if nobody asks me to sign theirs. Next year will be better. I'm going to be a better person and get to know everybody. This year doesn't count. So there.

I took my yearbook with almost a shudder.

You would not think yearbook signing could be traumatic. Trauma is living through tornadoes or divorce. And here I was so traumatized by what people might — or might *not* — write in my yearbook I couldn't even open the dumb thing.

Perhaps there was no picture of me. That would be a good excuse for not passing it around for signing.

Instantly somebody caroled, "Oh, there's a terrific shot of Alison right there in the candids on the third page. See her by herself at the piano?"

One of the boys said, "Where else?"

Everybody laughed, and I began thinking in terms of skipping my senior year. How did one go about getting early acceptance at college anyway?

First period was Chemistry. Our Chem teacher, universally disliked, is given to unfair, unannounced quizzes, which he so humorously refers to as "quizzicunies." I was just telling myself that even a dreaded quizzicunie would be better than yearbook exchanges when he said, "I'm feeling kind. You can spend the entire period on your yearbooks."

Kind. The fiend. I could pretend to be busy during two or three minutes of yearbook signing — but forty-four whole minutes?

Out of the corner of my eye I saw a sophomore boy approaching me. I had had precisely one contact with Jonathan outside of chemistry. He'd turned a page for me during an assembly last fall.

I smiled at him falsely. *Dear Jonathan,* I wrote, with my usual flair for yords. *Best wishes,* I added, before I could stop myself. Just what I never wanted anybody to write in my yearbook. Meaningless, blah junk anybody could write to anyone. I scribbled, *Wish you could turn pages for me more often.*

Oh God, I thought, that's even worse. That's so stupid. He won't even remember that.

I tried to think of something — anything — to add that would be funny or even sensible. I wrote, *Love, Alison.*

I couldn't believe that either. I didn't love Jonathan. I didn't even know Jonathan.

I would have destroyed the page if I could. But Jonathan had paid a lot of money for that yearbook and probably would press charges for destruction of personal property. There was nothing to do but hand it over. With a shaky smile I took my own back and we sat looking at each other, wanting to read what the other had written but afraid to. That ridiculous situation was resolved when our yearbooks were literally snatched out of our hands by other kids ready to exchange. I turned back to my desk. To my relief, it was stacked with yearbooks. There were definitely people out there, then, who wanted my name on my photograph.

Sue's was on the top. Sue, with whom I'd always wanted to sit at lunch but never had the nerve to invite myself. I took a deep breath. For once I put down exactly what I was thinking. *Dear Sue, I wish we knew each other better. Maybe next year. You always crack such funny jokes. At jobs I tell everyone your joke about the man with the extra shoe.* I reread it. It looked stupid, but there was no going back now. I lifted the next yearbook and wrote just what I thought there, too.

I told the people I admired why I admired them and I told the ones I didn't know very well how sorry I was I hadn't set up my schedule to fit in more friendships. The words upset me, seeing them written down, and I had no idea how anybody would take them. Would people laugh? ("Pitiful old Alison, begging for friends.") Or not even notice? ("Yeah, she signed mine. I think. I forget.")

But I felt better, somehow, expressing myself. I'd been uptight too long. Time to relax and say things to people.

I was feeling very good about myself right up through Latin, when Mike MacBride grinned at me. For many reasons, I could not relax around Mike. I liked him too much. And I felt so conscious of his being rightly disgusted with me.

Ms. Gardener called on me to translate third, and Mike fourth, and both of us relaxed about the Latin, at least, knowing we were safe for the rest of the class. Mike, who sits diagonally across from me, stretched out a long, plaid-shirted arm and grabbed my yearbook off my desk, handing me his. It would have been a fine, sneaky ploy except he dropped mine.

It bellyflopped on the floor during a total silence in which poor Frannie was trying to figure out whether the verb was in the subjunctive. Ms. Gardener said, "Michael? Could you and Alison consider paying attention to your Latin instead of to your already swollen egos?"

The class roared with laughter. I slid down in my seat. Mike just grinned and kept my yearbook. A few minutes later, when Ms. Gardener's back was turned, it got passed back to me.

Alison, he had written across his beautiful senior picture, ruining it from the pressure of his ball point pen, *very best wishes to you in the career that's obviously ahead. From an admirer, Mike MacBride.*

It was a nice, friendly, pleasant note.

I hated it.

What I wanted to write in his was, *Dear Michael, of all the boys in the senior class, you're the one I most wanted to date. It is not too late to remedy this situation. Love, Alison.*

But of course I didn't. You had to draw the line somewhere in this honesty stuff.

I considered writing this, *Dear Michael, I'll never forgive myself for spending so much time on music that I never even saw you play a single game. I've lost out on a lot at high school, from friendship to fun. Just hope it's been worth it.*

Well, that was even worse. Sounded as if I'd been pining away, lost and sorrowful, since sophomore year.

I tried to think of something just like what Mike had written. Perhaps, *Have a super year at college.*

I liked that. I bent over his yearbook to write it, but the space near my photograph was already filled.

I had written in it. The very words I'd decided I could not possibly put on paper.

Dear Michael, I'll never forgive myself for spending so much time on music . . .

I could not believe it. I wanted to rip the page out. I even got a grip on the page so as to rip it quickly and violently. Mike said, "Come on, Alison, the class is over. Just put *Love, Alison* on the end and hand it over, okay? My fans are swarming around demanding their turns."

I didn't have much choice. I wrote *Love, Alison* and handed it over.

I thought seriously of lying down on the linoleum and dying but I was too healthy.

Besides Mike wasn't even glancing at what I'd written. He was handing the book to Kimmy out in the hall.

The only thing worse than writing something absolutely humiliating is when the person you wrote it to doesn't notice it.

17.

Tuesday, thank heaven, made up for Monday and yearbooks.

When I got home from our combo rehearsal — we were learning a graduation march — there was a message scribbled on the pad by the telephone: *Call Ted, he wants to study at library with you Sat morn.*

Study at the library.

Now, over the years I have evolved a very definite study pattern. First of all, I only study in the afternoons. Nights are for gigs, and mornings, if I'm not off to school, are for staggering around trying to wake up.

Secondly, I believe a person can only study when she is sprawled out on her stomach on top of the bed with a bag of potato chips to eat and a radio blaring. The radio has to be close enough so that every time an ad comes on, she can jab a button and change the station.

It is impossible to study at a desk, sitting bolt upright, starving, thirsty, silent, and under observation by a steely-eyed librarian.

The sacrifices I am making for you, Ted, I thought, as I called him back. I had really gotten to like his number. The jingle I'd composed to sing the digits to was really terrific. Eight-six-nine . . .

"Can you really study in a library?" I asked suspiciously. I figured that what I would be studying was Ted.

"I have to. If I stay home, my mother gives me housework assignments. All week she's been making noises about how every spring the porch should be scrubbed and this spring it should also be painted. Believe me, Alison, I can study in a library. In fact, I may study there till it's time to leave for college!"

So we met at the library.

Ted picked our desk: neatly sandwiched between biographies and maps was a table for two, with a nice little divider so that the reference librarian could see us only if she walked all the way around the encyclopedias. "Considering the lady's weight problem," whispered Ted, "I doubt very much she walks around the encyclopedias more than once a year."

We talked about weight problems (his mother had one; I didn't) and about weight lifting (he liked it) and about going to college (he was wishing he'd decided to go somewhere else). "Listen," said Ted suddenly, as if I hadn't been, "I really do have to study."

"Okay. Sorry."

Ted began staring into the pages of his history text. I could practically feel him absorbing knowledge, his eyes focused on the page like laser beams.

I tried a little studying myself, but it wasn't the same without a radio and some potato chips, so I just sat and looked at the way Ted's hair fell on his forehead and thought about how he was going off to college a year ahead of me. That left us the summer.

I was not planning to get a summer job. I'd do whatever gigs came up — Ralph expected a slow season — and just laze around the rest of the time. I was sure that Ted was not the lazing-around-for-an-entire-summer type. Even if he were, his mother would change that. She sounded like an ogre!

Ted would probably be working full-time for the paper all summer. I wondered what his free-time schedule would be and whether I would fit into it.

At eleven-thirty, Ted looked at his watch, nodded sharply, took my wrist, put my watch next to his, observed that they both said precisely eleven-thirty, and said, "I am starved. It is time to eat."

"You sound like a first-grade reading text," I told him.

He answered me in short bouncy little syllables. "Ted and Alison go to lunch. See Ted go first. See Alison run after him."

We imitated the Dick-and-Jane style all the way home. Home — to Ted's house. I held my breath in nervousness; I was not really ready to meet his family — all those brothers and that ogre mother — but nobody else was home. We made ourselves sandwiches and took a jar of pickles and a bag of chips and sat on the back steps to eat.

The Mollison backyard was full of all the things he and his brothers had played on when they were little. Swings were still hanging from the limbs of huge oak trees; a rickety wooden ladder was nailed to the garage, leading to a treehouse precariously arranged between the garage roof and an oak; a basketball hoop was screwed into the garage wall low enough for a very little boy to get baskets with ease.

Ted was tall enough now to look down into the basket. I pictured him, my Ted, using that low basketball hoop. *My Ted.* I thought, But he isn't mine, really. Two or three conversations and a few kisses do not make a boy mine.

We kissed in the sunlight, scattering bread crumbs over our laps. "Can I pick you up after school Wednesday?" he said. "I'm free for the whole afternoon."

Could he!

Neither of us could think of anything interesting to do on a weekday afternoon, though.

"We could just do this," I suggested, and this time I kissed him first, and Ted laughed . . . and we did that.

"You like him, don't you?" said my father.

"Yes." One syllable and a heartfelt smile told it all. I didn't have to go on and on about it.

"You know, somehow," said Daddy reflectively, taking a kettle off the stove and pouring boiling water over teabags, "I thought it would be Michael MacBride you'd go around with. I think

139

you've like that boy since you were in first grade. I remember when Mike joined Cub Scouts, you came home every Tuesday to tell me how good he looked in his uniform and how many new badges he'd won." Daddy laughed and jiggled the teabags. You know it's summer when you start drinking your tea cold instead of hot. I added the lemon.

Yes, I could remember year after year of admiring Mike. Mike was romantic. I remember that in seventh grade particularly *all* the girls had crushes on him. It would have been practically un-American not to adore Mike. Athletic and elegant at the same time. On top of all that, such a nice person.

Even now, my head whirling with thoughts of Ted, the idea of Mike could make my thoughts whirl the other direction.

It threw me off completely. When I tried to practice I kept fumbling and missing notes. I threw the hit tunes aside and did some old Beethoven I hadn't looked at in a couple of years: great crashing chords that worked out so neatly in the end.

When Ted picked me up at school Wednesday, we drove to Mayberry's for ice cream. "Ted," I told him, "I don't have a weight problem yet, but if all we do every time we meet is eat something fattening, you'll have to shovel me in and out of your car."

Ted laughed. "I do that already." He disentangled the seat belt for about the hundredth time. "I tell you what," he said. "You just sit there and sip ice water. I'll have the chocolate sundae."

The only table empty was an awful, long, thin slab supposedly for two people. It was pressed up against the wall in the far corner, and the only decoration was some old plastic flowers in a red glass cup. We had so much table between us we had to hunch over the place mats and stick our necks forward like swans in order to talk privately. It was very uncomfortable. Ted's knees kept bumping into mine and the straw in my ice water kept getting caught in my hair.

"Alison?" Ted said.

"Mmmmm?" I was sneaking a bite of his chocolate topping.

"There's something I wanted to ask you."

"Sure." The chocolate was delicious. I lost my resolve to keep slim and began eating off my side of his sundae.

"You know," said Ted, "in your senior year, there are, you know, well . . ."

I got the straw out of my hair and rearranged our knees and leaned even farther across the table to hear his mutterings. "Senior year there are what?" I asked.

"Proms. Dances."

"Oh. I know. I've played for bunches. Are you going to be taking photographs of yours?"

"No. The yearbook is long done, sold, delivered, and autographed. No. I wondered if . . . if you'd go with me to our prom."

It had actually never crossed my mind that he would invite me to his senior prom. Somehow, our dates had seemed to me the sort that had to be squashed in between other, more important

141

things. So I was important enough to Ted to be asked to his senior prom! I was so delighted I actually clapped my hands. It would have been better if I had not been holding the spoon full of chocolate sauce and ice cream; the plastic flowers looked even worse with spattered chocolate on them. "I'd love to," I told him. "I can't wait. When is it?"

Ted's cheeks got more and more ruddy, and he occupied himself with cleaning up the flowers instead of looking at me. "Saturday," he said finally. "This Saturday."

"In four days?" I stared at him. He stared helplessly back at me, blushing. "I know I should have asked you ages ago," he said, "And I'm really sorry, I know you can't arrange anything that fast, or have a dress, or anything, and probably you have a gig anyhow, but I just didn't get around to asking you, that's all."

"Well, we can't talk about it over this crazy table," I said. "Let's go sit in your car. Of course I'm coming. I'd love to."

I thought about what Ralph was going to say. Nothing good, that was for sure. We had a big date. I almost prayed to Ralph, as if he were God, not to mind if I went with Ted instead of to a gig.

We sat in Ted's car and laughed at each other and talked about getting tuxedoes and dresses. "Actually," said Ted, "I can't dance, which is one reason I felt so edgy about asking you."

"I don't dance very much myself. Let's go over to my house and practice."

Before we left for my house, we practiced kissing a little bit, too. For a moment I didn't want *anything* between us, not an ice cream table, not even a sweater. The prom, I thought. I finally have a real date for a dance. With Ted!

18.

"Saturday night?" said Ralph. "*This very Saturday night?* But we're doing a prom ourselves at Catholic High!"

"Please, Ralph?" I pleaded. "Can't you call that guy who does the gigs when my father won't let me go?"

There was a long silence on Ralph's end of the phone.

My heart sank. Ted and I had both agreed that if Ralph could not find a sub for me I'd have to play in the combo and not go to the prom. I felt a dreadful headache starting. Oh, how I wanted to go to the dance with Ted! How awful it would be to have to sit all night at somebody else's prom, providing them with music to dance by, knowing Ted was home alone.

"I suppose," said Ralph at last, "that it would be good for you to dance instead of work for a change. All right. I'm probably a soft old idiot, but all right. Go. Have a good time."

"Oh, thank you!" I said to him over and over. "Thank you!"

I hung up, called Ted, and yelled to Daddy to see if he wanted to go shopping with me to buy a prom dress.

I expected Daddy to tease me and tell me to call a girlfriend and just laugh at the whole idea of his going prom dress shopping. But he didn't even answer me, and when I tracked him down in the kitchen he was sort of leaning up against the cabinets and there were tears in his eyes. "Daddy," I said, astonished, "what's the matter?"

"Oh, kitten. I'm sorry to be sad in the middle of all your fun. I don't think about your mother much, really. It's been so many years. But something about our little daughter going to a prom. I just looked at her photograph and I hurt all over, wishing she could be here to do that with you."

He walked away and I didn't follow him. I stared at the flowers growing in our neighbor's garden and thought about how mixed up the universe was, when I could be totally thrilled about one evening out of three hundred sixty-five that year, while my father was weeping for a person neither of us really remembered.

I thought about my mother for a while, and I wondered if she had gone to proms and ached over boys and worried whether or not my father loved her.

Prom dresses.

Who would have thought there could be so many tacky, dull, misshapen, and out-of-style prom dresses hanging on the racks in so many stores? By the time I actually managed to start

145

shopping (would you believe Saturday morning?) every shop I went to was empty of anything decent.

Ted said he didn't know what I was worried about; why didn't I just wear that midnight blue satin number with the cutout lace sleeves? I tried to explain that there was no way I'd be caught dead in a performer's spangled costume when I was going as his date, but he didn't understand at all. In fact, my father really didn't understand either.

"Let's see," said the saleslady at one store, looking me over carefully. "We'll want something very demure and simple for you, dear. That's your style." She dredged up something that looked like a nightgown and something else that looked like a housecoat. Terrific. It was almost lunch and I had not yet found a dress.

I was supposed to meet Ted for lunch and have the dress with me so he could figure out what kind of corsage would match it. I had a feeling that Ted knew zero about corsages. He'd probably say to the florist, "I don't know. She's wearing something bluish. You choose."

I hobbled over to the restaurant where we were meeting. (All I had to show for a morning of shopping was a beginning blister on my heel.) The restaurant was not at all what I had expected. It was dark and expensive and full of middle-aged adults who should have been dieting. I wondered if Ted had ever eaten there before.

A tall, thin waiter in a white dinner jacket asked what party I was with. "Um," I said nervously. "Ted Mollison, please."

And he led me to a table where no Ted Mollison sat. An enormous woman (who *definitely* should have been dieting) was taking up most of the space. She turned out to be Ted's mother.

"Oh," I said weakly. The ogre who suspected musicians of scandalous things. Oh, God. "Hi," I added.

That was the absolute total of things I could think of to say.

"Hello, dear," said Mrs. Mollison. She beamed at me and took my hand to pull me down into her triple chins for a squishy hug. "Did you find a dress? No? Well, after lunch, you and I will go to the Katydid Shoppe. You've never been there? It's perfect for you. Now. What will you have to eat? You're dieting? Nonsense, you're positively frail. Have the seafood platter, it's delicious. I've been known to order two at a time. Ted? Oh, he's coming, he just had to run some errands for me. I told him we wouldn't wait and he wasn't surprised. When it's food, Alison dear, I hardly ever wait!" Mrs. Mollison burst out laughing and I couldn't help laughing with her. Ten minutes later we were old buddies. She was as comfortable and easy to be around as Ted — although considerably more of her was around. Ten minutes after that I was actually telling her about my father being upset because my mother couldn't go prom dress shopping with me and Mrs. Mollison said she understood perfectly, and I thought she probably did, too.

By the time Ted arrived, panting with exhaustion from running all her errands, we were finishing up coffee and dessert and having such a good time telling each other stories that Ted complained about feeling left out.

His mother beamed at him, gave him a suffocating hug, and excused herself to "go freshen up." (I've always thought that was such a funny phrase, as if you'd gotten stale and moldy over dinner.) Ted began talking where his mother had left off and I thought, No, no Mollison would get stale and moldy. They're too full of themselves and all the things they're doing and going to do.

Ted peppered his London broil lavishly. I told myself to remember that: Ted uses a lot of pepper. I felt as if I were keeping a mental notebook on Ted, filing away things that helped me get to know him better. I flipped mentally through the pages. A lot of blank ones, I thought, giggling to myself. Plenty of space to write more.

Mrs. Mollison and I left Ted with his steak and salad and went off to the Katydid Shoppe, and she was right: They had perfect dresses. Everything I tried on felt just right. We finally settled for a pale blue cotton dress with row upon row of lavendar, blue, and white embroidery. It was a country, peasant type of dress. A more complete change from what I usually wore to dances could not be imagined. I didn't feel like a musician when I wore it. The skirt was full and frothy, and the little off-the-shoulder sleeves were lacy and girlish.

I'll wear my hair down, I thought. No braids, no stars, no spangles. Just thick waves and curls.

Tonight I will not be a keyboard man!

"Oh, Alison!" said Ted when I came downstairs, and that was all he had to say. I felt like spun candy: special and light.

Ted felt the same way he always did: solid, comfortable, crinkly, and nice.

The dance was wonderful.

It was so odd to be the dancer. Not worrying about the next request. Not caring about whether the electric guitar lost power or the trumpeter had a toothache. Every now and then I'd glance over to the orchestra and just smile for the sheer pleasure of *not* being in it. "You miss it?" said Ted once. "You wish you were up there?"

"No!" I said emphatically.

"I kind of miss my camera," said Ted. "There are a lot of good shots here. Somehow photography is always at the edge of my mind. I sort of see things in frames."

"I know what you mean. I feel the chords coming for the modulation they're about to do on-stage. The drummer was rushing a little back there and I felt that."

We talked music and photography and what we wanted to do with our lives. Ted wanted to go on to some really prominent paper, not the little punky (as he said) *Register*. Maybe the *Washton Post* or *The New York Times*. I told him about wanting Nashville and cutting records.

I met Ted's friends — he had a lot of them; I envied him — and we ate and talked and danced with so many people. I really did feel like Cinderella at the ball, whirling every second.

At midnight we walked outside. Western High has a courtyard planted with slender saplings, dotted with cement benches and urns full of flowers. We stood in a corner and it was too dark to see each other; but then, we didn't really need to see. Outside, away from it, the music was nothing but a throb echoing how we felt about each other.

I knew I would enjoy it when Ted put his arms around me, but I was not prepared for how *much* I would enjoy it.

They're just arms, I told myself . . . but they weren't. They were more: They made me feel hot and wild. When we kissed again Ted had stopped being his old comfortable self, and we were pressing fiercely against each other. Ted pushed my hair away from my neck and kissed my throat and for the first time in my life I really wanted the kisses to go on forever.

We stood back from each other, sort of gasping for breath, and I said shakily, "Oh, Ted."

When we walked back in we were like strangers, not touching. It was as if we had gotten so close for a moment that we'd burned each other. It was scary.

19.

Ted telephoned the next day around noon. "You up yet?" he said.

"Mmmmm. Sort of." Sunday, I thought. I had no plans for Sunday — no music, no homework, no nothing.

"Can I come over?"

"Sure. I'd love to see you." I got up and brushed my teeth and slapped some cold water on my face. Last night had taken a lot out of me!

I could scarcely remember what we had done after we came back into the school at midnight. There had been noise and talk and wild dancing and lots of laughter. I had been so dizzy from thinking about Ted that a lot of it just hadn't registered. We'd gone on to an after-prom supper by somebody's pool and dragged ourselves home around three in the morning.

I stared at the hollow-eyed face in the mirror. How could anybody like her!

We had actually been too tired to kiss good night. In fact, I think both of us were too tired to *wave* good night! I had staggered up the stairs and fallen asleep half-undressed, lying on top of the covers. Daddy's breakfast-making noises had waked me up around seven and I'd finished undressing and slid between the sheets to sleep another few hours.

Lunch, I thought. It's lunchtime. Have to make something for Ted to eat.

The June sunlight poured in our kitchen windows. It was so warm and pleasant there. My father had gone to get the morning papers at the drugstore. I sat listening to the refrigerator hum. How will I feel when Ted comes? I thought. Hot and on fire? Or relaxed and comfortable?

I began shaping hamburger patties.

When Ted rang the bell, my hands were all greasy from handling the meat. It actually upset me to keep him waiting the half-minute while I washed and dried my hands. Wow, I thought, laughing at myself, have I got it bad!

We hugged hello. Ted was his solid, ordinary self. He was wearing an old workshirt and cordury pants with a tear below the knee. I was in jeans and an embroidered sweatshirt instead of an evening gown and satin slippers. There was no music and no atmosphere — and my heart flipped over just the way it had at the dance.

Oh, Ted, I thought. Is this just a crush or do I love you?

My father came in with the Sunday morning papers and we sat reading the comics together, laughing, and then we tried to work the crossword, and then I declaimed every line from the one article in there that Ted had written. (It was

about a school board meeting where nothing happened, and we had the best time making every
sentence dramatic and intense with hidden meaning!)

Is it Ted who is special? I thought. Or am I just
so delighted not to be a musician at a keyboard
that that's what I'm in love with?

It was the last day of school.

The seniors had come back to get their report
cards and certificates. They stood on the huge
marble front steps of the school, looking so much
older than the rest of us who would be coming
back for another year. A group of boys and girls
clustered around each other, hugging good-bye.
They were going off to jobs and college. They
kept crying out things like, "Oh, Jimmy, I may
never see you again!" and, "Why did you have to
decide to go to a college on the west coast, anyway?"

I may never see them again either, I thought.
For a moment I hurt all over, thinking of lost
chances to be friends with these people, thinking
of the tricks of time and geography that separated
people who had once shared everything from
lockers to jokes.

One of the group was Mike MacBride.

He detached himself from the others and came
over to me, smiling his quiet, elegant smile. I
knew I had never met anybody as good-looking as
Michael MacBride. He really was a perfect man.

Man, I thought, half-shivering at the word. Yes,
he had graduated and was no longer a high school
boy, but a man.

A man, I thought with a pang, that I hardly know.

"How are you, Alison?"

"Fine. How are you?" Such dumb things to be saying to somebody you had admired your whole life. "Your picture in the yearbook was so good," I managed.

"Thanks. Yours was very dramatic, sitting there at the keyboard as if you're about to give a spectacular concert."

I had laced two narrow braids of hair at my temples and pulled them gently to the back and tied them with a ribbon. Mike lifted one of the braids with his finger and stroked it. "You wrote in my yearbook that high school was ruined by not seeing any ball games," said Mike. "Want to un-ruin your record and go with me to one next Saturday?"

Mike, whom I'd adored for years, asking me out. Giving me another chance to get to know him.

I'm not actually officially going with Ted, I thought. We haven't made each other any promises. I could perfectly well go to a ball game with Mike. And Ted hadn't asked me out for Saturday.

In the back of my mind I could hear Ted's voice, see Ted's face, feel Ted's arms.

I swallowed. "Oh, Mike, you're super to offer. I . . . I'd love to. But . . . but I'm dating a boy from Western and I can't. Thank you anyway. I . . . it's really nice of you." My stutterings dwindled away.

Mike merely smiled at me again and the smile tore at me. Am I doing the right thing? I thought desperately.

Mike said gently, "Have a nice summer then, Alison," and he walked off and I knew I would probably never see or hear from him again, what with his summer and college plans.

My chest hurt and the backs of my eyes prickled with tears. I walked home, because I had missed the last bus. The sun was streaming yellow, but I felt gray, bleak, and lonely.

A horn beeped twice behind me.

I recognized it. Ted! I thought, before I even turned, and my gray mood lifted. When the car pulled up next to me, I was grinning widely, and Ted was grinning back that crinkly, comforting smile — and I knew I had done the right thing.

"Where'll we go, Alison?" said Ted, kissing me quick and moving back into traffic.

"I don't care," I told him.

And I didn't. Anywhere he wanted to drive was fine with me, as long as we were together.